You're invited to a

CREEPOVER ®

The Terror Behind the Mask

written by P. J. Night

SIMON SPOTLIGHT
New York London Toronto Sydney New Delhi

This book is a work of fiction. Any references to historical events, real people, or real places are used fictitiously. Other names, characters, places, and events are products of the author's imagination, and any resemblance to actual events or places or persons, living or dead, is entirely coincidental.

SIMON SPOTLIGHT
An imprint of Simon & Schuster Children's Publishing Division
1230 Avenue of the Americas, New York, New York 10020
First Simon Spotlight paperback edition August 2014
Copyright © 2014 by Simon & Schuster, Inc.
All rights reserved, including the right of reproduction in whole or in part in any form.
SIMON SPOTLIGHT and colophon are registered trademarks of Simon & Schuster, Inc.
YOU'RE INVITED TO A CREEPOVER is a registered trademark of Simon & Schuster, Inc.
Text by Kama Einhorn
Designed by Nick Sciacca
For information about special discounts for bulk purchases, please contact Simon & Schuster Special Sales at 1-866-506-1949 or business@simonandschuster.com.
Manufactured in the United States of America 0714 OFF
10 9 8 7 6 5 4 3 2 1
ISBN 978-1-4814-0460-0
ISBN 978-1-4814-0461-7 (eBook)
Library of Congress Catalog Card Number 2013940838

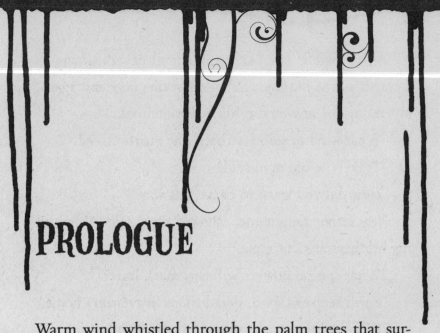

PROLOGUE

Warm wind whistled through the palm trees that surrounded the old man's carving studio. Chunks of fresh coconut lay on his worktable, where his large, leathered hands slowly and carefully moved a small knife across the surface of a piece of wood, stained red. He was creating something from nothing, giving life and a soul to a piece of wood. Making it into something else, something powerful . . . a mask.

The old man had worked for several days, stopping only to rest on a mat on the ground, eat the food his visitor brought him, and chant his prayers. At night, far-off drumbeats sounded, and moonlight shone through the tiny openings in his palm-frond roof.

All the while, his visitor quietly observed, sitting in a corner of the hut and asking questions now and again, scribbling the answers in his little notebook.

"What kind of wood is that?" the visitor asked.

"Teak," the old man said.

"How did you learn to carve this way?"

"My father taught me," the old man said. "Me and my brothers at same time."

"What special powers will this mask have?"

"It will keep evil spirits and demons away from a home."

"Who will the mask belong to?" the visitor asked.

The old man smiled. "To you, my guest," he said. "It will be a gift to you."

The visitor put his hand on his own chest in gratitude, as if touching his heart. He had just hoped to observe the mask-maker. Now he was being given a great honor.

The mask-maker began to carve the eyes. He had saved them for last. He used a special tool, and hummed as he cut the eyes from the wood. Wood shavings fell to the ground below, quickly blending in with the grains of sand. They were now one with the earth.

Once the eyeholes were big enough, the old man put down his knife. He studied his work. The face he had created was contorted into a grimace with a furrowed brow. Its smile was wide and toothy, its nose long and beaklike. The expression carved in the wood was both angry and worried.

Now it was time to give the mask its powers. The old man picked up a small worn glass bottle from his work-table. He poured a bit of oil from the bottle onto his hands and rubbed them together carefully but briskly, until the oil was warm between his palms. Then he lovingly massaged the oil onto the mask, chanting quietly. When he was done, he closed his eyes and held the mask in both hands and sat silently for a few minutes. He could feel the mask's power growing, coming alive.

Then the old man proudly turned the mask around to face his visitor, so the visitor could see it too. The visitor smiled and nodded. He wasn't just being polite; he was clearly impressed. And then . . .

Snap! Click! Flash! Snap! Click! Flash! The sound and light from the visitor's camera filled the quiet, shady studio. The old man stared hard at his visitor and spoke each of his next words as if each were an ax chopping through wood:

"No photos. Not of the mask. Ever."

Snap! Click! Flash! The visitor did not stop taking

photographs. The old man growled another warning.

"Do not make me ask you again!" His voice was low and rumbly, like thunder. "Capturing the mask has terrible consequences."

Again: *Snap! Click! Flash!*

The old man threw the mask down onto the sandy floor as though it burned him to the touch. He stood up at his carving table, held up one leathered hand, and knocked his supplies onto the floor. "I warned you, but you did not listen," he bellowed. "You have summoned evil. The Booga spirit has been awakened."

He lunged for the visitor's camera and grabbed ahold of its strap. Then he banged it again and again onto his empty worktable. The lens cracked, and several black plastic pieces broke off, sinking into the sandy floor.

The visitor stared, shocked. Without another word, the old man stomped out of the hut and into the bright sunlight, leaving the mask behind.

The visitor reached down to pull the mask from the sand, and held it in his hands. Sand clung to the wet oil on the mask. The visitor sat down again, back in his corner of the hut. He set the mask on the ground once more and put his head in his hands. What had he done?

CHAPTER 1

Jasmine Porter always read before she went to sleep. It felt great to slip into bed, turn on the reading light clipped to her headboard, and open a book. It was like entering another world. And she usually fell asleep while reading.

Tonight Jasmine would start a book her dad had bought her on one of their father-daughter book-buying sprees before he went off on his latest trip. They always went to the same neighborhood bookstore, Bookworm, and her dad always said the same thing: "Pick out what you want, Jazzy-Jas." And he really meant it. Jasmine could choose twenty books, and her dad wouldn't even blink in surprise. He'd just smile, take them from her, and plop them down at the register.

"Really?" she'd sometimes say when she'd gone on a particularly large binge. "I can have all of them?"

And her dad would always say the same thing: "You can't put a price on the pleasure that reading gives."

It was true: they both loved to read. Sometimes they would sit on the couch for hours, both immersed in their own books, and not say a word to each other. The only sound in the room would be of pages turning.

That's what it was like as Jasmine lay in bed reading. It was just her breathing and the sound of pages turning. The bulb of her reading lamp was so bright, she could actually feel its heat. After a few chapters, Jasmine's eyes grew heavy, her grip on the book started to loosen, and she knew she should close it, turn off the reading light, put the book on the night table, and face the truth: she would finally have to give in to sleep.

Jasmine reached up and turned off the reading light, but instead of going dark, the room was still bright. Jasmine looked up and noticed that the overhead light was on. She got out of bed and walked, bleary-eyed, toward the light switch next to the door, and flicked the switch.

But as the room went dark, Jasmine quickly realized that she should have turned the reading light back on first, because now it was pitch-black, unless you counted the glow-in-the-dark stars on her ceiling, which didn't exactly provide any real light (though they were pretty). Where was the little night-light that was plugged into the outlet? It usually gave off a soft glow and made Jasmine feel so much better.

As much as she hated to admit it, Jasmine was afraid of the dark. And she really liked that night-light. It was made of orange and yellow glass and shaped like a baby owl, and she'd had it since she herself was a baby. *The bulb must've burned out,* she thought. The last few times that had happened, she'd called out to her dad, who had come in and changed the bulb. But her dad was still away on his trip, and Jasmine was alone in the house with her grandmother, who Jasmine knew would already be asleep.

Jasmine sighed. It seemed like her dad was always gone at the wrong times.

Sometimes he would try to talk to her about his having to travel a lot for work, as if he was fishing for her real feelings about him being gone. "Did you have any dreams while I was away?" he'd ask, as if that would give him some clue to her deepest thoughts. Or he'd say,

7

"When I was your age, I hated it when my mom went back to work and left me home alone a lot." It was like he expected Jasmine to immediately join the conversation and confess her true feelings.

And Jasmine just wasn't going to do that. She also wasn't going to tell her dad how scared she still was of the dark, or about the little rituals she believed kept her safe at night. Every night for the past three years, she'd whispered, "You're okay," to herself three times and made sure the covers were pulled up all the way to her ears before she would close her eyes. She also wasn't going to tell him she thought that maybe he'd traveled the world enough, and that maybe it was time to stay put and be a real parent, like, full time, no joke.

So whenever her dad tried to start a conversation like this, Jasmine pretended she was someone else—someone who didn't care. And she'd shrug or roll her eyes.

Now Jasmine stood in the dark at the light switch. She could turn the overhead light back on, walk to the bed, flick on the reading light, and then come back. But that would set her back from falling asleep. No, she could do this.

Jasmine tried to let her eyes adjust to the dark so she

could see a tiny bit, just so she could make her way back to bed without tripping and falling on her face. And, of course, so that she could keep a close eye on the closet as she passed. Because the idea of something being in that closet—something that was going to get her—was so real to Jasmine that she feared it deep in her bones.

"The bogeyman" didn't quite do it justice, nor did "monster." Both names sounded childish compared to what she actually feared.

When she was younger, she'd made her dad check the closet before she'd gone to sleep. He'd always reassure her that there was no such thing as the bogeyman, and that there were no monsters in the closet. Jasmine's dad always humored her by opening the closet door and looking around first. But now that she was older, she was embarrassed to ask him to check. Still, she was too afraid to check herself. Instead she settled for staring at the closet door, making sure it didn't creak open and release some horrible, evil . . . thing.

The basic outline of the room was starting to reveal itself to Jasmine's tired, anxious eyes. The light creeping in from the hallway was helping a bit. Jasmine knew it was time to walk past the closet and jump quickly into bed.

She tentatively crept forward, still afraid of tripping in her messy room. *One foot in front of the other, one foot in front of the other,* she chanted in her head. She kept her eyes on that closet door, as if by sheer will she could keep it closed and keep herself safe from whatever was inside.

It felt like forever, but Jasmine finally made it back to her bed. And there she was, standing at the side of it, ready to crawl under the covers to safety, when suddenly she felt something grab her around her left ankle.

A cold, slimy grip. It felt like something between a hand and a claw. And then it began to pull, *hard.*

Jasmine struggled desperately to keep her balance. The thing wanted to drag her under the bed. And no matter how hard she tried, Jasmine couldn't keep her footing. She lost her balance and fell to the floor.

Then the actual dragging began. A force much stronger than she thought possible was pulling her. It was like the time she had been swimming in the ocean and gotten sucked under the waves. But that time her dad had been there to pull her back to safety. Jasmine focused on that memory, rather than the feel of the rough carpet burning her leg as she was dragged under the bed.

CHAPTER 2

Jasmine's head bolted up off her pillow. Though she was covered in blankets, she was cold. She slowly realized she was covered in something else. Sweat. Yuck. She looked at the clock on her bedside table: 4:25. The little blue numbers glowed innocently, bringing Jasmine back to the real world. "It was just a dream, just a dream, just a dream," Jasmine repeated in a hoarse whisper. "You're okay. You're okay. You're okay."

She settled back down and closed her eyes. *There has to be a word for this moment*, she thought. The moment you realize that the something terrible that just happened was only in a dream. *Relief* didn't quite seem to cover the joy Jasmine felt at being free from that slimy grasp. As her terror slowly faded, her sleek black cat, Momo, jumped onto the bed and curled up against Jasmine's leg. It was the cat version of a comforting hug. His purring was like a lullaby that miraculously put her right back to sleep.

The next time Jasmine opened her eyes, it was to the *beep beep* of the alarm and sunlight filling her room. Once she turned off the alarm, she even heard birds chirping outside. It was as though the darkness of night had never been scary, and nothing would ever be scary again. If only!

Jasmine sighed and swung her legs onto the floor. The day had officially begun. Time to shower.

As she stood under the hot water and woke up more, she began to remember her nightmare in detail. She closed her eyes and imagined washing the nightmare away. But no matter how hard she scrubbed with the bar of soap, the unease clung to her like a layer of dirt.

At least it was Friday. Her best friend since preschool, Lisa, would be sleeping over tonight. They had sleepovers almost every Friday night, either at Jasmine's house or Lisa's. It was easy, because Lisa lived right down the street. The two girls lived in the same New Orleans neighborhood. Jasmine loved her city—everywhere you went you heard music and laughter and you smelled delicious food cooking. That was especially true of Jasmine's own house. Her grandmother was famous around the neighborhood for her jambalaya, a spicy rice and sausage dish. Whenever her grandmother made it, she always cooked enough for all the neighbors.

Momo used his nose to poke the bathroom door open and keep Jasmine company as she combed her wet hair. "Hello, little panther," said Jasmine. Momo was sleek and beautiful, and he reminded Jasmine of a black panther she had seen in a nature show on television. Just a few years ago she had even imagined that he was secretly just a panther cub and one day he'd be huge. But Momo was just an ordinary, skinny black cat, though he was very sweet. "Silly panther baby," she laughed as Momo jumped onto the tub and began lapping at the drops of water still dripping from the faucet. He did that all the time.

Jasmine's grandmother was at the kitchen table with her coffee when Jasmine came downstairs.

"Hi, Nana," Jasmine greeted her as she spread butter on the toast that Nana had put out for her. Nana never seemed to eat breakfast; she just drank coffee. Or maybe she ate after Jasmine left. Jasmine didn't know. In any case, she usually sat with Nana in the morning before school, just the two of them, because Jasmine's dad traveled a lot.

Like, a *lot*. In fact, traveling was his actual job—he was a travel writer. He wrote magazine articles about the places he'd visited. And it seemed like he'd been just about everywhere. "On assignment" was what he called it. A magazine would assign him an article about a certain place and off he'd fly.

As much as Jasmine missed her dad, she did enjoy her time with Nana. Nana cracked Jasmine up. She was full of superstitions, like "If you have a headache, tap your head three times with a potato"; "Make a wish on a quarter moon"; or "Wear a safety pin on your collar for good luck." Jasmine didn't know where any of this came from, but it was what made Nana, Nana. Nana was a little spacey, but she was very loving. Plus, she made yummy food.

"I hope I told you," Jasmine said to Nana, putting down her toast and beginning to unpeel a banana. "Or maybe Dad told you before he left. Lisa's sleeping over tonight, okay?"

"Of course, dear." Nana smiled. "Lisa is family."

It was true. "Like peanut butter and jelly," her dad would say sometimes when looking at them together.

"Or red beans and rice," Lisa would add. That was her favorite food. Jasmine had to agree—she and Lisa went together so well, it was like they were made to be best friends.

There was only one thing about Lisa that Jasmine didn't like, and it had developed pretty recently. It was Lisa's new obsession with ghost stories. She read every scary book she could get her hands on and always wanted to talk about them with Jasmine. Lisa just seemed to love scary stuff, while Jasmine would just as soon never hear the words *haunted* or *ghost* ever.

And Lisa had started really creeping Jasmine out when they were sleeping at Jasmine's house. During the last few sleepovers, Lisa had told Jasmine there were "cold spots" in the house—random areas that never heated up even when the heat was fully on. Jasmine had never noticed them before, but now she did, of course. Also, whenever they heard a strange noise, Lisa would raise her eyebrows triumphantly as if to say, *See? Ghosts!*

Lisa knew very little about Jasmine's fears of the dark or ghosts or the bogeyman under the bed or monsters in the closet or pretty much everything else that went bump in the night. If Lisa did know, she wouldn't be torturing Jasmine like this. But Jasmine didn't want to admit her fears to anyone—not even her best friend—because in the light of day she knew that they were just that: fears in her head. Not real.

So far, Jasmine had been able to ignore Lisa when she got into one of her ghostly moods. She figured that if she didn't respond, Lisa would eventually stop. Like if you had a roaring fire in the fireplace, but you wanted it to go out, you wouldn't add any more logs to it. As Jasmine sat and finished her breakfast, she silently hoped that Lisa wouldn't add any more fuel to the fire tonight.

CHAPTER 3

On the bus to school, Jasmine began to relax for the first time all morning. School would be bright, crowded, and predictable. Just what Jasmine needed. But as she looked out the window, she replayed the dream in her head. She didn't want to do this, but she couldn't help herself.

It was as if the nightmare were a ghost haunting her brain. She tried to think about happy things, like how her dad was coming home tomorrow or how Lisa would be sleeping over tonight and they would watch a movie (and it would *not* be a scary one, if Jasmine had anything to do with it).

Jasmine was glad when the bus pulled up to the big

sign in front of her school: MONROE MIDDLE SCHOOL: THE PRIDE OF NEW ORLEANS.

First period was English, which Jasmine and Lisa had together. They sat next to each other too, because their teacher, Ms. Berger, let her students choose their own seats in the beginning of the year, which most teachers didn't do. She was lots of kids' favorite teacher.

Even if you didn't know them, Jasmine and Lisa looked like best friends. They wore the same backpack but in different colors (Jasmine's was lime-green, Lisa's was turquoise), had the same stickers on their notebooks, and even clipped the same barrettes in their hair (because they had split one package of four pairs). English was also both girls' favorite class. Ms. Berger had a special way of making whatever they were reading come alive.

As everyone wandered in and took their seats, Jasmine and Lisa were both busy reading the board.

Ms. Berger wrote one on the board every morning before her students entered the classroom. Then she'd have the class talk about the day's quote for a few minutes before they began their lesson. Today she had written:

"No man, for any considerable period, can wear one face to himself, and another to the multitude, without finally getting bewildered as to which may be the true."

—Nathaniel Hawthorne

Jasmine really liked Mardi Gras. It was a big two-week party that happened every year in New Orleans, with fabulous costumes and colorful masks and parades with giant floats and parties and food. And the beads! Pretty, colorful beaded necklaces piled on one after another. And the tourists—people came from all over the world to celebrate Mardi Gras in New Orleans. The city turned into one giant festival.

"Good morning, everyone," called Ms. Berger, clapping her hands to get the class's attention. "Who wants to read today's quote out loud?" No one raised a hand. Ms. Berger scanned the room. "Jasmine?" she said, looking right at Jasmine.

Jasmine looked at the quote on the board and nodded. "'No man, for any considerable period, can wear one face to himself, and another to the multitude, without finally getting bewildered as to which may be the true. Nathaniel Hawthorne,'" she read.

"Thank you, Jasmine," Ms. Berger said. "First of all, *multitude* means 'crowd,' like the public. Okay. Who has something to say about this quote?" Again, no one raised a hand.

Ms. Berger laughed. "Let's try this again. Good morning! Nice to see everyone so wide-awake! Who can tell me what this quote has to do with Mardi Gras?"

A boy named Nick raised his hand. "Well, it talks about wearing one face or another face. So maybe it's sort of about wearing masks, like people do on Mardi Gras?"

"Aha!" Ms Berger said. "Glad to know someone's awake on this Friday morning. Yup, the quote doesn't use the word *mask*, but metaphorically, that sure is what Nathaniel Hawthorne was talking about. Remember our discussion about metaphors?"

Jasmine remembered. Metaphors were a way to describe something by comparing it to another thing, such as *your brain is a superfast computer* or *her smile is a gleaming string of pearls*.

"So how is this quote a metaphor for a mask?" Ms. Berger asked.

Lisa raised her hand and got called on. "If you act

one way when you are alone and another way when you are around others, it's as if you're wearing a mask. Like you're hiding your true self," she said. "After a while, you might get confused about which is your real self. So maybe you shouldn't have two faces; maybe you shouldn't wear a mask. Wearing a mask is like being phony."

"Good, Lisa," said Ms. Berger. "Masks are a very powerful metaphor, and we're going to be seeing a lot of masks around our city during Mardi Gras, so you could take that opportunity to think about what masks might symbolize. It might just have something to do with your own life. So, on that note, and to kick off the Mardi Gras season, I want to introduce you to the first two stanzas of the new poem we will be studying, which is 'We Wear the Mask' by Paul Laurence Dunbar." Ms. Berger removed the first quote, and then pulled up a poem onto the board.

We Wear the Mask

We wear the mask that grins and lies,
It hides our cheeks and shades our eyes,—
This debt we pay to human guile;

With torn and bleeding hearts we smile,
And mouth with myriad subtleties.

Why should the world be over-wise,
In counting all our tears and sighs?
Nay, let them only see us, while
We wear the mask.

—Paul Laurence Dunbar (1872–1906)

"Paul Laurence Dunbar," Ms. Berger said, "is often called the first major African-American poet in America. His parents were freed slaves from Kentucky. And he was one of the few African Americans of his time who spoke honestly about what he saw around him. Okay, there's clearly a lot to discuss here, and this is only a part of the poem. But first, a little vocab lesson. *Guile* means 'sly intelligence' and *myriad* means 'many,' like too many to count. Now, let's have a feeling survey," she announced. Ms. Berger usually did this after reading a poem, to see how it made everyone feel.

"Who feels sad after reading this?" Ms. Berger asked.

A few kids, including Jasmine and Lisa, raised their hands.

"Who feels mad?"

Again, a few kids raised their hands.

"Does anyone feel happy or peaceful, like everything is okay?" she asked. No one raised his or her hand.

"Okay, so we know the words made us feel mad and sad, but let's dig deeper and figure out why," Ms. Berger said. "First, a little context. Between which years did the poet live?"

A girl named Maxie raised her hand. "1872 to 1906," she said.

"Okay," Ms. Berger said. "I know in your history class you're studying that period, the period right after the Civil War. Who can tell me what life was like for African Americans then? Did their lives instantly get better because slavery ended?"

Most kids shook their heads.

"Right," Ms. Berger said. "Times were tough in America then. The war had ended slavery, and African Americans *seemed* to be in a better situation than before. But the truth was, things still weren't all that great for them. So the poem is about African Americans pretending to be content with the way things were. The poem is about trying to cover up the painful truth—that they were feeling pretty rotten and unable to talk about their feelings in an honest way. Raise your hand if you're with me," she added.

Most kids raised their hands.

"Are the people in the poem *really* wearing masks?" Ms. Berger asked.

Everyone shook their heads again.

"That's right. So in this poem, masks are a . . ."

"Metaphor," everyone said.

"Yes," Ms. Berger said. "Excellent. Now, someone explain that metaphor in their own words."

Lisa raised her hand. "The masks mean that the people in the poem are hiding something," she said. "They are covering up their true suffering."

"Why do we wear masks at Mardi Gras?" Ms. Berger asked. "For fun, because they're pretty, or to pretend to be someone else for a while. With a mask, we get to pretend, right? But imagine having to wear a mask all the time. And I think you can. Because everyone has a mask that they wear at least sometimes—one that hides their true feelings. The poem's meaning isn't limited to African Americans. It speaks to everyone.

"It took courage to write this poem," Ms. Berger continued. "It took courage for Dunbar to speak up about his real feelings. And that inspired many other African American poets. Now I want you to think about the metaphorical mask *you* wear sometimes. What are *you* covering up? What kind of mask do you cover it up with? What would *you* like to speak up about? Open your journals and write for five straight minutes. Start by copying one line of the poem, whichever one speaks to you the loudest. Then just write your personal reflection about that line—whatever comes out. No one else will read it but you, so be honest."

Jasmine opened her notebook. She noticed her hands were kind of shaky. Still, she picked up her pen and copied one line of the poem:

We wear the mask that grins and lies.

Then she wrote:

I wear a mask too. My mask looks brave, independent, and cool. I pretend to be fine when Dad is away. I pretend it doesn't bother me when he leaves. I pretend not to be afraid of the dark. I pretend not to freak out when Lisa talks about ghosts and haunted houses. I pretend I'm tough and can take care of myself. No one knows what I hide behind my mask. I even have Dad and Lisa fooled. Now that is totally depressing.

The bell signaling the end of the period broke through Jasmine's sad thoughts.

"Okay, time's up," Ms. Berger said. "Excellent work. Have a great day, guys."

CHAPTER 4

English class had definitely been intense, especially because it was first thing in the morning. But much to Jasmine's relief, the next part of the day was fun and easy. In study hall, which came just after first period, kids got to choose and sign up for "mini-courses" that would take place on Monday. Mini-Course Day happened once every marking period. On Mini-Course Day every teacher in the school taught something he or she knew a lot about or something he or she knew well but did not teach in their regular classes. Every student got to spend the day in his or her choice of special classes. On the previous Mini-Course Day, Jasmine had taken cake decorating and tie-dyeing, and the year before, karate and hurricane science.

Jasmine looked at her sign-up form. There were so many good topics to choose from this year. Jasmine narrowed her choices down to "Juggling and Magic Tricks," "Mardi Gras Mask-Making," "Learn a Little Japanese," and "Crash Course in Shakespeare."

"Let's do the mask one together," Lisa said. "It'll be fun, and we can wear the masks to the parade. Otherwise we'll just end up buying them in a store like we always do."

"I may have had enough of *masks* for one day," Jasmine said, and groaned, but she was only kidding. It actually sounded like fun, and she liked arts and crafts kind of things. She circled "Mardi Gras Mask-Making" and "Learn a Little Japanese" on her form. Learning Japanese would be fun too, she figured. She'd surprise her dad with what she learned, since he'd been there and also knew some words. Then she went to her next class, math.

The rest of the day was totally ordinary. She and Lisa ate lunch together with their usual lunch buddies, Lily and Nina, and they all traded food, as they always did. Jasmine and Lisa were happy to learn that Lily and Nina had signed up for "Mardi Gras Mask-Making" too, so they would all be together. When the day ended,

Jasmine felt pretty good, and last night's nightmare had disappeared from her brain.

As her bus pulled up in front of her house, Jasmine noticed a taxi in her driveway. What was this? Her dad wasn't supposed to come home until the next day. But there he was, lugging his bag out of the trunk, paying the driver, and turning around with a huge smile on his face as Jasmine got off the bus.

"Jazzy-Jas!" he called, holding his arms open for a big bear hug. Jasmine ran into them and, even though it seemed kind of babyish, put her head on his shoulder and said happily, "I missed you, Daddy!"

"I missed you too," her dad said. "I caught an earlier flight. I thought I'd surprise you. Surprise!" He laughed.

"You did surprise me," Jasmine admitted happily. "You'll be surprising Nana, too."

"Let's go do that then, shall we?" Her dad grinned and picked up his suitcase. He always traveled pretty light. It was something that, as a professional travel writer, he prided himself on. He could be ready to go anywhere at a moment's notice.

"I brought a gift for the whole family this time," he added as he and Jasmine walked up the steps that led to their front door. Because their home was actually at sea level, their basement was above ground and their living area was above that. "I'll show you when we get inside."

Jasmine grinned. Her dad always picked out the best presents. He brought her home a little something from each of his trips. Sometimes it was as simple as a handful of coins from the country he'd visited. But even that was special. She'd think about the actual people living so far away who'd used the coins and held them in their hands, or had them in their pockets or wallets.

But Jasmine thought about it as they entered the house and felt a little disappointed that her dad hadn't brought back a gift especially for her. She had to share her dad with the whole entire world, and now she had to share his presents, too? Oh, well. She told herself she was acting kind of spoiled.

Her dad plopped his suitcase on the couch and unzipped it. He dug in deep to pull out a package. It was about the size of a large plate, wrapped in newspaper and lots of tape. Nana brought in a pair of scissors.

Jasmine's dad paused dramatically. "This was a gift

to me from my hosts," he said. He suddenly looked very serious. "It was made by an elder of the tribe. It was a great honor to be given this."

Jasmine eagerly cut through the tape and carefully pulled back the newspaper. But she stared down in horror at the contents of the package. A wooden mask. Red. She cautiously touched it with her fingertips. It felt warm and smooth, but that was about the best thing Jasmine could think about it. It looked like the bogeyman—her bogeyman. The face of the mask had a strange, gigantic smile, one that made it look like it was in some sort of pain. Its eyebrows were all bunched up. Its nose looked like it belonged on a cartoon bird. Its eyes, even though there were just holes, still seemed somehow crossed, as if they were trying to look at each other. The mask had an expression that was mad and worried at the same time.

"The tribe I visited believes that a mask like this protects a house from evil spirits and watches over the people in it," her dad said. "And if an evil spirit does come near your door, you just put on the mask, and the evil spirit will be scared away. The mask-maker learned the art from his father, who learned from *his* father, and on and on, maybe even thousands of years ago." Her father gazed at the mask as if it were the most beautiful thing he'd ever seen.

"It took the mask-maker days to make it," he continued. "And I watched him the whole time. There is something I feel a little badly about though." He had a faraway look in his eyes. "I took a picture of him making the mask, and he didn't like that, but I couldn't stop myself. It was just so interesting, and I wanted to show other people what he looked like as he made it and what it was like inside his carving studio. But now I wish I had stopped when he asked. . . ."

Jasmine looked at her father. He had kind of drifted off into his thoughts. She gave him a little pat on his arm.

Her dad chuckled. "Sorry about that. But I think I can turn that bad experience into a good one," he said. "This mask will always remind me to respect the wishes of the people I write about."

Jasmine, her dad, and her grandmother stared silently at the mask. Soon Jasmine's dad turned to Jasmine and searched her face, trying to read her expression, which was sheer horror.

"What's the matter, Jazzy?" her dad asked. "You're not scared, are you? You know there's really no such thing as evil spirits. It's just a superstition."

Jasmine's heart felt like it was sinking into her stomach. The memory of last night's nightmare came flooding back. The cold slimy thing that had grabbed her ankle now felt like it was clutching her heart tightly.

She had a terrible feeling that she would always be alone in the world, no matter who was there with her. Alone with her fears. And she would always be scared of the dark. She would always have to watch the closet door. And now, she'd have to live with this big face, with this horrible-looking expression, looming over her.

This mask was going to *watch over them*? That was the last thing she needed, thank you very much.

Nana had already left the room to get a hammer and nail. "Where would you like to hang it?" she asked Jasmine and her dad.

How about nowhere? Jasmine thought.

"How about at the top of the stairs?" Jasmine's dad suggested.

Nana nodded.

"Why don't you help Nana while I wash up and unpack, Jazzy?" Jasmine's dad suggested. "I'm going to try to get through dinner without falling asleep. Think I can make it?"

Jasmine didn't respond. She silently followed Nana up the steps and watched as Nana *tap-tap-tapped* a small nail into the wall. Then she hung the mask on the nail. Nana didn't really need Jasmine's help. It was as simple as that. As simple and as horrible.

This day sure was full of masks, Jasmine thought, staring at the crazy wooden face that was supposed to protect her but instead gave her the chills. *And this mask is the worst of all.*

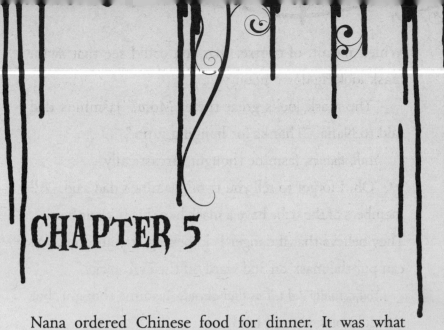

CHAPTER 5

Nana ordered Chinese food for dinner. It was what Jasmine's dad always liked to have when he came home from one of his trips.

"You just can't get good Chinese food where I was," he would always say. (Except, of course, after he came back from China. He'd raved about the food there and said it was pretty different from the American version of Chinese food.)

Jasmine was an expert at using chopsticks. Her dad had taught her how long ago. He'd said it was "an important life skill to have." The three of them sat at the dining room table, which was located in such a place that you could see the top of the stairs when you were sitting.

Which meant, of course, that you could see that awful mask looking down upon you.

"The mask looks great there, Mom," Jasmine's dad said to Nana. "Thanks for hanging it up."

Yeah, thanks, Jasmine thought sarcastically.

"Oh, I forgot to tell you two," Jasmine's dad said. "All members of the tribe have a mask like this in their homes. They believe that if danger is knocking at your door, you can put the mask on and ward off the evil spirits."

You actually did tell us that already, Jasmine thought, but she did not say it out loud.

Jasmine's dad looked over at her. "It's just a legend, Jazz," he added. "I got a kick out of the idea that you two would be protected by the mask when I'm away on assignment. Not that you need protecting," he said quickly. "You're two very strong, smart, sensible, and independent people."

Jasmine could tell her dad added that last part because his suggestion that she and Jasmine needed protecting was quickly offending Nana. Nana took great pride in taking care of Jasmine and keeping the house safe. She had raised six kids by herself without a lot of money after her husband had died when the kids were little.

She would remind Jasmine and her dad periodically that she didn't need anyone to protect her. She could take perfectly good care of herself and her family.

Jasmine thought this would probably be a great time to change the subject. "So how long are you home for?" she asked her dad. She knew to ask this close to when he got home, because chances were he'd be off again soon. He loved his work and hardly ever turned down an assignment. He didn't seem to mind the long plane trips, and often traveled with his photographer friend, Buddy. A lot of Buddy's photos were displayed in their home, actually. Jasmine wished one of the photos were at the top of the stairs in place of the mask.

Whenever Jasmine's dad got home from a trip, he'd spend day and night at his computer, typing on the keyboard loudly, as if getting his notes into the computer was very urgent. And maybe it was. He had important, interesting things to write about each place he'd visited, and obviously his readers agreed with him, because his office walls were covered in travel writing awards and honors.

He used his chopsticks to reach for some more moo shu. "A few days, actually, honey," he said. He looked carefully at her face for signs of disappointment. Jasmine didn't show any, of course. She was good at wearing her own mask.

"This is a big one," her dad added. "I'll be going north of the Arctic Circle for the very first time. It will be super-cold. I'll be in a remote part of Russia called Siberia."

"What will you be doing there?" Jasmine asked politely.

"I'll be living with native hunters for a few weeks," he answered. "I'm going to observe how they trap animals for food and fur, and how they build their boats from trees, and how they make their own skis to travel around in all the snow. They're expert craftsmen, and the world doesn't really know about their work. It's very hard to get there. The only way is by boat, helicopter, or dogsled. I'm very lucky they agreed to host me."

"Wow," Jasmine said, trying to keep her true feelings out of her voice. She knew her father's work was interesting and fascinating and all that, but the only thing she could think was *Gee, could Siberia be any farther away from home?*

As if reading her mind, Jasmine's dad pulled out his phone and tapped the map app. "I'll show you exactly where it is," he said. He showed her a world map and pointed at a line that sort of went across the top. "That's the Arctic Circle," he said. "It's actually an imaginary line. You learned about longitude and latitude in school, right? See, the Arctic Circle covers Russia, Canada, Alaska, Greenland, and parts of Scandinavia. So now let's zoom in on Siberia, which is part of Russia, and *here's* the little village I'll be visiting." Jasmine took the phone and looked carefully. She loved that map app, the way it was like you were an astronaut way out in space and then you were slowly landing on Earth.

"What about you two?" her dad asked. "What do you have planned? Mardi Gras is just around the corner, isn't it?"

"The days just fly by," Nana said. "Well, Jasmine and I will make our special king cake, as always."

Jasmine thought her grandmother's king cake was pretty cool. It was like a giant cinnamon roll with purple, gold, and green sugary icing. Those were the three colors of Mardi Gras. But here was the really cool thing: a tiny plastic baby doll was placed into the cake, and whoever got the piece with the baby was supposed to host the party the next year. Jasmine and Nana had changed this tradition into "whoever gets the plastic baby doll doesn't have to clean up the mess we made while baking."

"I'll be sorry to miss that this year," her dad said, smiling. "You guys should open your own bakery for Mardi Gras. Seriously. Your king cakes are *that* good."

Jasmine smiled. "Yeah. Our bakery could be called Jazzy Nana."

"Or Nanny Jazz," Nana added with a chuckle.

"And what about parties or parade plans?" Jasmine's dad asked. "Anything brewing yet?"

"I'm not sure. I'll be making a mask in school on Mini-Course Day. And some kids from school will be having parties, I think." Jasmine looked away from her dad and, unfortunately, the mask caught her eye again.

"What are you thinking?" her dad asked her.

Nana raised her eyebrows.

"You really want to know?" Jasmine asked her dad, a little edge to her voice. As soon as the words came out of her mouth, she regretted them. Now she might have to actually tell him.

"Of course," he answered. "You can always tell me what you're thinking."

"That mask totally creeps me out," she admitted, pointing to the top of the stairs without looking up.

Her dad nodded, a sympathetic look on his face.

"What about it creeps you out?" he asked.

"Um, I guess its expression," Jasmine said, her voice getting softer. "That expression on its face. It just looks so freaky and so creepy. I don't know. Never mind," she said quickly.

"I hear you, Jazzy," her dad said gently. "And I do agree its expression is kind of strange. I wish you could have met the people in this village, though. They were so generous, even though they had very little themselves. They were a very gentle, peaceful people. They shared everything with me and made me feel like such an honored guest. You know, Buddy wasn't with me this time, so I was taking my own photos, and they were very gracious about it, letting me take pictures of the children and everything. And of the mask-maker himself. Well, except for in the very end, when he got mad at me for taking the pictures of the mask, he was such a kind and lovely man."

"Why did he get so mad?" Jasmine asked.

"I'm not totally sure, actually," her dad said. "I can only guess. Actually, there's an anthropologist I can talk to about it. I have to call him about the article anyway. He's an expert on that tribe, and he may be able to help explain what happened."

"Oh," Jasmine said. "What's an anthropologist?"

"There are lots of different kinds of anthropologists, but the one I'm thinking of studies cultures and the people within them," her dad said. "To learn about how they live. Some anthropologists specialize in certain cultures, like the guy I'm going to call. Anyway, the mask is in good company. It's hanging with all our family pictures."

Jasmine knew, of course, that practically every inch of the wall was covered in family photos both old and new. Her favorite one was of her and her dad when she was about one year old. They were at a pumpkin patch, and Jasmine's dad was helping her sit on top of a pumpkin that was about the same size as she was.

Jasmine really wanted to change the subject again. "Oh, there's another thing going on in the next few weeks besides Mardi Gras," she said. "The animal shelter is having a fund-raiser and I'm making cat toys to sell." Jasmine volunteered once a week at a shelter for cats and dogs, the one where they'd found Momo. She cleaned cages, brushed the cats and walked the dogs, and helped get them ready to be adopted. If a cat was shy, she'd spend extra time with it to get it more used to being around people.

"That's great, honey," Jasmine's dad said. "Do you have everything you need?"

"Yeah," Jasmine said. "They're giving me all the supplies. Including the catnip that's going inside each toy!" She tried for a carefree laugh. "They're going to sell them for five dollars each," she added.

"Time for fortune cookies," Nana said, handing one to both Jasmine and her dad. Jasmine had been so wrapped up in her conversation with her dad that she hadn't even noticed that they had finished eating. She opened the plastic wrapper and cracked hers in half right away. She loved fortune cookies. She examined the little strip of white paper silently as she chewed the sweet, crunchy cookie. *I can't wait till Lisa gets here for our sleepover and I can forget about all this mask stuff,* she thought. Lisa would be arriving just after dinner.

"Mine says, 'All your hard work will pay off,'" Nana announced. "Now, I like that! But it already has," she added, looking proudly at her son and granddaughter.

"That's a good one," Jasmine's dad said. "Mine's pretty great too. Listen to this. 'You have a way with words.' How do you like that! Well, I should hope so; otherwise I'm out of a job!"

43

Jasmine and Nana laughed. But then Jasmine frowned.

"Well?" her dad asked. "What's your fortune, Jazzy?"

Jasmine kept staring at her slip of paper and didn't respond.

"Are you okay, honey?" Nana asked.

"I'm fine," Jasmine said, looking up.

"Well?" her dad asked again.

Jasmine looked back down and kept her eyes on her fortune. She didn't look at her dad or grandmother. "It says, 'The only thing we have to fear is fear itself. Franklin Delano Roosevelt.'"

Jasmine was glad that this wasn't one of Ms. Berger's quotes that they would have to discuss the meaning of. She'd had enough of her own fears for one twenty-four-hour period—of feeling them, of thinking about them, and of talking about them.

Her dad leaned back in his chair and slowly clapped his hands a few times. "Well, there you go, Jazzy."

CHAPTER 6

Dingdong. Dingdong. Finally! There was Lisa was at the door, sleeping bag in hand. Jasmine and Lisa headed upstairs right away.

But at the top of the stairs, Lisa stopped in front of the mask. "Wow," she said, looking up. "This is really freaky and also kinda cool. Where did it come from?"

"My dad just brought it back from his trip," Jasmine mumbled. Then she stayed silent, even though Lisa was clearly waiting for more of a response. Jasmine didn't want to encourage Lisa to talk about the mask—she was going to try to pretend it wasn't there. But of course Lisa kept asking questions. She was practically acting like a newspaper reporter. She touched the mask gently with her fingertips.

"Who made it? Did your dad say?"

"Um, an old guy," Jasmine answered. "He gave it to my dad. Come on, let's go to my room."

"Wait a second," Lisa said. She moved in closer to the mask to get a better look. Jasmine took a step back.

"Sometimes masks like these have special powers," Lisa said casually, as if she were talking about the weather. "Like magical powers. I saw a show on TV about it. Does this one? Did your dad say?"

"He mentioned something about what it's supposed to do, I guess," Jasmine admitted. "But I wasn't really paying attention. Come on."

Lisa followed Jasmine to her room, much to Jasmine's relief. But she kept asking: "So does it, does it?"

"Does it what?" Jasmine said flatly.

"Have special powers!" Lisa's whole face was lit up with excitement.

Jasmine sighed. "If I tell you, will you stop asking?" she finally said.

"I promise!" Lisa said, and held her right hand over her heart.

"Okay, but seriously, you need to stop. It's just some boring travel story my dad came back with, as always,"

Jasmine said. "The mask is supposed to protect a house from evil spirits. Okay?"

Lisa stared solemnly at Jasmine. "How does it do that?" she asked.

"Aaaaargh! I don't know!" Jasmine said, her voice rising with annoyance. "You said you'd stop asking!"

"Okay," Lisa finally said. "Do you want to watch TV?"

"Yes, please!" Jasmine laughed. She was lucky enough to have a television in her bedroom, after years of asking her dad for one. They watched a movie about twins who switch places and trick everyone. It was pretty good. When it was over, Jasmine handed Lisa the remote. "Here, you can choose."

Lisa flipped through a bunch of shows that Jasmine actually wanted to watch, but she reminded herself she had told Lisa she could choose the channel. "Yay!" Lisa crowed, stopping on a show called *Haunted New Orleans*.

Jasmine groaned. That was pretty much the last thing she wanted to watch with the exception of *Haunted New Orleans and Especially That Creepy Mask in Jasmine Porter's House*. The host of the show had a very deep and spooky voice. Jasmine knew the producers of the show were just trying to set the mood, but she wished they wouldn't set it so well.

This episode took place in an old home in the French Quarter. The owner was being interviewed.

"Well, when I bought the building, there were stories," the owner was saying. "But I didn't believe any of them. The price was so low that I just had to buy the place. It wasn't until after I started renting rooms out and people began coming to me, inquiring about strange goings-on, that I started to rethink my decision."

Jasmine couldn't take it anymore. She grabbed the remote and turned the channel. Some silly game show came on.

Lisa grabbed the remote and turned it back to the ghost show. The owner was still talking. "Like cold spots, spots in the house that wouldn't heat up. And noises at all hours of the day or night even when no one else was home or everyone was asleep. Things like that."

Jasmine grabbed the remote from Lisa's grip and turned the channel again.

"You are being such a scaredy-cat!" Lisa laughed. "Come on, this stuff is so fun."

"I am not a scaredy-cat," Jasmine protested, although of course she knew the truth about herself. "I'm just in the mood for doing something else."

"All right, scaredy," Lisa teased. "What do you want to do, then? It's almost time for lights-out."

Nana still had a very strict "bedtime" for Jasmine, though the girls were allowed to talk while they lay in bed in the dark.

"I don't know," Jasmine said softly. She felt kind of badly. She hated to ruin Lisa's fun, but that show was just too scary for her. It was going to give her nightmares—she just knew it. "We could play a game online," she suggested.

"Or we could plan our own Haunted New Orleans episode!" Lisa said, her eyes bright. "After your dad and Nana go to sleep, we could search for ghosts in your house. Because you know my theory . . . There are ghosts in this house."

Jasmine sighed dramatically, trying to cover up her dread of actually playing the game Lisa had suggested, as well as the sinking feeling she got whenever Lisa wanted to talk about how she thought there were ghosts in her house.

"And you know what else," Lisa went on, "I read somewhere that New Orleans is the most haunted city in the United States."

"Really?" Jasmine had never heard such a thing. Just her luck.

A sudden overwhelming feeling of sadness enveloped Jasmine. She tried to keep a normal expression on her face. *Me and my mask,* she thought.

But Lisa was still chattering away. "There are lots of reasons why New Orleans is so haunted," she said kind of dreamily. From history class, and from just living in New Orleans, they both knew that their city was settled by the French beginning in the 1690s and that many of the houses, including those in their neighborhood, were very old.

"Lights-out!" Nana called from downstairs. *Great,* Jasmine thought. *Just in time for me to freak out about being in the dark. As usual.* She got up and turned out the light just as Lisa crawled into her sleeping bag on the floor. The two sat silently in the near dark for a minute.

Creak! Jasmine jumped a little, but it was just her dad opening the door and poking his head into the room. "Good night, girls," he said in a singsong voice. "Sleep tight. Don't let the bedbugs bite!" Jasmine was secretly annoyed whenever her dad said that rhyme, which was often. Why would he put such a horrible thought in her head just when she was getting ready to sleep? Little bugs in your bed that came out when you were asleep. *And bit your skin!* But Jasmine tried to keep her voice light and steady as she said "Good night, Dad."

"Good night, Mr. Porter," Lisa said.

"Lisa, how many times have I told you to call me Martin?" Jasmine's dad scolded in a joking way.

"Good night, Martin." Lisa laughed, and Jasmine was jealous of how natural Lisa's laugh sounded—she would fall right to sleep, while Jasmine predicted that she'd lie there wide-awake thinking about ghosts and the bogeyman for a while. She was glad the night-light had been fixed. She had casually asked her dad to replace the bulb earlier, and she was relieved that he had. He left the door open a crack so some of the light from the hallway spilled in. Jasmine heard him enter his study down the hall and start up his computer.

Sometimes it seemed like he never stopped working.

Lisa was already breathing differently, the way you do when you're asleep. Again, jealousy rose in Jasmine's chest at the ease with which her best friend fell asleep. *She is probably dreaming of unicorns and puppies and lollipops and rainbows,* Jasmine figured. Jasmine lay patiently and waited for sleep to come. But something strange started happening.

Jasmine's hands and toes felt like they were falling asleep, all pins and needles. She hated that feeling. And the blanket was feeling heavier and heavier on her body. *Maybe I should get up,* she thought. Whenever she complained about her arm or leg falling asleep, her dad would tell her to move it around as much as she could to "wake it up."

Jasmine quietly got up and tiptoed out of the room, stepping carefully over Lisa in her sleeping bag. The hall was bright, thankfully, and she walked slowly to the bathroom, trying not to disturb her dad working in the study.

The bathroom door was closed, which it usually wasn't, and Jasmine turned the handle and opened it and . . .

HISSSSSS! HISSSSSS! The sound reached Jasmine's ears before she processed what she saw. *HISSSSSS!* And when Jasmine was finally able to focus on what was in front of her, she wished she had kept her eyes closed.

CHAPTER 7

The mask—the mask that her father had just brought home, that she had just seen hanging at the top of the stairs—was a foot in front of Jasmine's face. And it wasn't just a mask.

It was attached to a gargantuan snake. The snake was coiled and piled on the bathroom floor like a giant piece of scaly rope. Its body completely filled the room. Everything started moving in slow motion as Jasmine turned around and ran from the bathroom, closing the door behind her and running toward her dad's study.

But the creature had left a slimy trail on its way to the bathroom that Jasmine's feet stuck to like glue. She couldn't move. Before she even knew it, the snake burst through the bathroom door and speed-slithered right up to her. Part of it was still in the bathroom, but its head—the mask—was right in front of Jasmine's face again. It was shaking around like a hideous, gruesome, gigantic bobblehead doll.

Then the mask flew off the snake and fell to the floor with a loud clatter.

And what Jasmine now saw in front of her was more horrifying than the mask itself.

Because the snake had no head at all.

Jasmine saw just a bloody stump where its head *should* have been. Veins hung out like pieces of wet red yarn. Blood pulsed out of them and onto the floor. But somehow the snake still hissed. *HISSSSSSSSS. HISSSSSSSSS.*

"Daddy!" Jasmine screamed. But the hissing was so loud that even Jasmine couldn't hear her desperate screams for help.

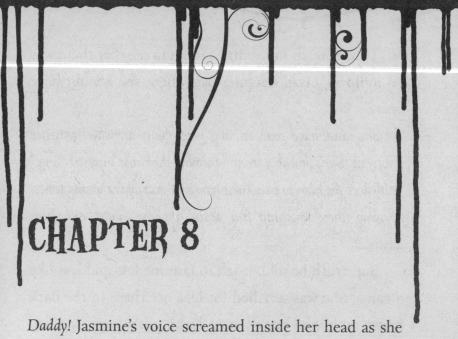

CHAPTER 8

Daddy! Jasmine's voice screamed inside her head as she sat straight up. She looked at the clock on her bedside table. The little blue numbers said 4:25. Somewhere in the fog of Jasmine's mind she remembered waking up from her nightmare at that exact same moment last night. *It was just a dream, just a dream, just a dream,* Jasmine repeated in her head, suddenly aware of not wanting to wake Lisa up. Instead she mentally said what she always said: *You're okay. You're okay. You're okay.*

She automatically looked around for Momo, who always made her feel better after she had a nightmare. But no Momo. Where was Momo when you needed him?

And Momo wasn't the only one who wasn't there. It

was light enough in Jasmine's room to see that there was no lump in Lisa's sleeping bag where she should have been.

She must have gone on that ghost hunt anyway, Jasmine thought. *She's probably creeping around the house "investigating." Why does she have to play these games at exactly the wrong times? Anyway, there's nothing fun about a ghost hunt—anywhere, anytime!*

But, truth be told, it felt to Jasmine less and less like a game. She was terrified for Lisa out there in the dark house with who-knows-what lurking. At once she had two thoughts, making her want to bury herself under the covers and never come back out:

1. The nightmare was some kind of warning that *something* was lurking in the house.

2. She had to go look for Lisa and bring her back to safety. It was the only right thing to do.

Jasmine got out of bed, feeling sick to her stomach. Every cell of her body told her not to leave her bed. But Lisa! What about her best friend out there with some headless masked monster? Jasmine would never forgive herself if something happened to Lisa. It was like the "buddy system" that her teachers used on field trips when they were younger: Everyone had a buddy, and you watched out for your buddy at all times. If your buddy got hurt or you couldn't see your buddy, you told a teacher right away. Whenever they went on a field trip, Lisa and Jasmine were buddies. *If only there were someone to tell, someone who could help,* Jasmine thought. But Jasmine didn't want to have a "talk" with her dad about her fears. She was getting too old to go running to Daddy or Nana every time she was scared.

Jasmine walked slowly downstairs. So far, Lisa was nowhere in sight, but Jasmine had an idea where her best friend would be. The basement. Lisa was always saying that the cold spots were most noticeable down there.

Jasmine's bare feet were cold. Moonlight filled the first floor of the house. She went into the kitchen where empty Chinese food containers had been rinsed and left on the counter. It seemed like so long ago that she had sat and eaten with her dad and Nana. She opened the cabinet under the sink to find the flashlight. There it was. She turned it on to make sure it was working. It was. She kept it on. *I need all the light I can get,* she thought.

The basement door was right off the kitchen, and it was open. Jasmine shone the flashlight down the steps. *Put one foot in front of the other,* she told herself. *For Lisa, your best friend.* She put her foot down on the first step. *There you go. One more step. One more step.* She was concentrating on not falling down the stairs, which was a welcome distraction from other, more disturbing thoughts. She shone the flashlight on her foot and the next step. Finally she was at the bottom. The cement floor was cool and dusty under her feet. Her heart beating wildly, she slowly moved the beam around to search the room.

And in a far corner of the basement she saw it, shining in the beam of light.

The mask! And it was moving! Silently thrashing around in the dark with its crazy smile and furrowed brow. Even in all its writhing, its eyeholes never lost their focus. They stared right at her. And then Jasmine saw it. One of the eyes in the holes winked.

The next sound Jasmine heard was not the hissing she had heard in her nightmare. It was her own voice, screaming.

Screaming. Screaming. Screaming. And everything began happening in slow motion. Her screaming could have been going on for two seconds or two minutes, maybe even two hours. Jasmine had no clue. She only continued to scream, too terrified to turn her back and run upstairs.

Then—no more mask. Instead there was Lisa's face in front of Jasmine's, twisted into a mixture of laughter and guilt. She held the mask in her hand, at her side.

"It's only me!" She laughed.

Jasmine sat down right on the cold cement floor, brought her knees up, buried her head in them, and covered her head with her arms. She concentrated on breathing. She wasn't even able to look at Lisa, who kept repeating, "It's only me. It's only me!"

A trick. Her best friend in the world had played a trick on her. A dumb, mean, thoughtless trick. Jasmine got up, a little dizzy from standing too fast.

Jasmine had felt pure fear when she saw the mask moving wildly in the darkness of the basement. And now she felt something else just as strongly—fury. Pure fury. She stared at Lisa. Her anger was so strong, she almost believed that her eyes could bore holes right into Lisa's head.

Lisa stared back with a nervous smile. She held up the mask in front of her face again and jiggled it in the air a little. "See, it's only me!" she said again, laughing. Then she stopped. She seemed to realize she'd gone too far.

Well, it's a little late to realize that, Jasmine thought. Jasmine walked quickly up the basement stairs and through the kitchen. She heard Lisa behind her, but she just walked faster.

"Jazzy!" There was her dad, a panicked look on his face.

Her screaming must have woken him up. *And the night just keeps getting better,* Jasmine thought sarcastically.

"Sorry, Dad," Jasmine said quickly. Suddenly she was embarrassed. "Everything's fine."

"Really? It didn't sound fine," her dad said, putting a hand on Jasmine's shoulder. "Where's Lisa?"

Just then Lisa appeared. She followed Jasmine's lead. "Sorry, Mr. Porter," she said. "We were just playing around."

"It didn't sound like play. You scared me half to death." Jasmine's dad sighed. The three stood there in awkward silence. "What were you two doing in the basement at this time of night?"

"We're sorry," Lisa said. She was holding the mask behind her back, not wanting Jasmine's dad to see it.

Jasmine's dad sighed again. "Okay, I'm going back to bed, and I strongly suggest that you both do too."

Jasmine pushed past her dad and ran upstairs. She couldn't get into bed fast enough. She was already there and under the covers when Lisa entered and silently crawled back into her sleeping bag. The two lay in silence. There were no words for Jasmine's anger. And her heart was still beating so fast.

Jasmine stared at the glowing constellations on the ceiling. When she and her dad had put them up, they had arranged them in the shapes of actual constellations, like the Big Dipper and the Little Dipper. And there was Orion, the hunter.

When she finally spoke to Lisa, Jasmine's voice was low and even. "We are totally not going to be speaking for a long time."

Lisa said nothing in reply. Was she asleep already? Jasmine turned to look at her. Lisa's eyes were open and she was staring at the ceiling too.

"Get it?" Jasmine asked Lisa. Her voice was hard around the edges.

Lisa had an odd grin on her face, like she was about to crack up, laughing. "Why are you talking to me? I thought we weren't speaking," she said. She seemed to think that this whole thing was hilarious.

"You thought right," Jasmine said, and turned over, putting her back to her best friend. She hugged her extra pillow and closed her eyes tightly. *You're okay. You're okay. You're okay.*

CHAPTER 9

When Jasmine opened her eyes the next morning, the first thing she saw was Lisa's face just a few feet away from her. Lisa was sleeping deeply and peacefully, even though the room was already bright with sunlight. Jasmine stared down at Lisa's face with its light dusting of freckles.

Then, in a rush, she remembered what had happened last night, both the nightmare with the snake and then the real-life nightmare that her "best friend" had put her through. Jasmine's heart beat faster as she remembered the way the mask had taunted her in the flashlight's beam, and the way Lisa had laughed and said, *It's only me. It's only me!* As she remembered all the details, Jasmine didn't take her eyes off Lisa's face. She stared at it as if she could send thought waves directly through her friend's face and right into her brain. And the thoughts were: *How could you do that to me? I thought you were my best friend!*

Jasmine suddenly wanted to wake Lisa up in the most unpleasant way possible, like by pouring a glass of ice water over her head. *Two wrongs don't make a right,* she reminded herself, one of Nana's favorite expressions. Jasmine kept looking at Lisa's face, as if searching for clues that would explain why Lisa had been so cruel with that trick last night. Jasmine was hot and thirsty— usually two good reasons to throw back the covers, go downstairs, pour herself some cranberry juice, and start the day. But she stayed in bed, frozen with resentment as she continued to stare at Lisa's face.

As though jostled by Jasmine's thoughts, Lisa began to stretch and move as she awoke. Jasmine kept staring. She wanted to witness that moment when Lisa first woke up and didn't know where she was. And then she did. Lisa flinched as she felt Jasmine's eyes on her. She was disoriented and groggy.

"Oh, *hello,*" Jasmine said sarcastically.

Lisa made some sleepy murmuring noises and closed

her eyes again. "Hi," she said, smiling slightly, completely missing Jasmine's sarcasm.

"Have a good sleep?" Jasmine asked Lisa loudly and slowly. "I sure hope so. Because I'm never going to sleep well again."

Lisa yawned and fixed her gaze upon Jasmine. "Oh, calm down," she said, stretching her hands above her head and wiggling her fingers. "Can't you take a joke? I didn't think you were such a scaredy-cat."

Jasmine gave an indignant chuckle. Then she felt the anger from last night, hot and real. "Leave," she said simply. Flatly.

Lisa ignored her. "Hey, do you think your dad got beignets?" She smiled. Beignets were the girls' Saturday morning treat when Jasmine's dad was around. He'd go and get the special fritters at the bakery in the early morning, and if they woke up at a reasonable hour, the beignets would still be warm.

How could Lisa be thinking about beignets? "*Beignets?*" Jasmine said in disbelief.

"Yeah, beignets," Lisa replied innocently.

Another wave of anger washed over Jasmine, and suddenly she couldn't bear to have Lisa in her room—or in her *house*, for that matter—another second.

"Leave," she commanded again.

Lisa sat up and looked at Jasmine as if she were being unreasonable. But Jasmine felt perfectly reasonable.

"Leave. Just leave," she repeated.

Lisa sighed, got up, and began getting dressed, gathering her things, and rolling up her sleeping bag. Suddenly it seemed that Lisa wanted to get out of there as fast as Jasmine wanted her gone.

Jasmine waited until she heard the front door close, which it did, although *slammed* was probably a more accurate word. She's *mad at* me? Jasmine thought. *Talk about ridiculous.*

Finally Jasmine got up and made her way toward the first floor. She stopped at the top of the stairs: there was the mask, crookedly hanging in its spot. Lisa must have put it back on the wall on her way upstairs last night. How thoughtful of her. Jasmine tried to not look at it.

Her dad was having coffee at the breakfast table. And there were the beignets. Jasmine sighed and plopped down in her chair.

"Quite a night, huh, Jazzy?" her dad asked with a sympathetic smile. "Lisa sure left in a huff just now." He seemed to have gotten over it. If only Jasmine could say the same.

"Uh, yeah," Jasmine mumbled, grabbing a beignet and taking a big bite. "Subject change, please."

"You got it," her dad said. "What's going on for you this weekend? Any plans?"

"Nope," Jasmine said. "Just homework."

"Okay, honey," her dad said. "Well, enjoy your breakfast. Please excuse me. I've got a phone call to make."

Jasmine finished her beignet and brushed the powdered sugar off her hands and onto her pajamas. The morning sun filled the kitchen. She glanced at the door that opened to the basement stairs. The terror of last night seemed like it happened forever ago. And it also felt like it had just happened only moments before. But mostly what Jasmine felt now was sad. She was still mad at Lisa, but sadness was quickly taking over. She sighed again, got up slowly, and started up the steps to her room. Maybe she'd go back to bed. As she passed her dad's office, she heard a voice on speakerphone. Her dad did lots of his interviews for his articles this way because it allowed him to type with two hands as he listened to whomever was on the other end of the call.

". . . may have believed that your camera was stealing something from the mask," a man's voice was saying.

"I've heard of that," Jasmine's dad said. "But I've never heard of it in this tribe."

"More study is certainly needed," the voice said.

"But, Dr. Wilson," her dad began tentatively, "he didn't seem afraid. He was angry. Said that I'd summoned some evil."

"So it could be that his mask-making was a ritual," Dr. Wilson said. "And you taking pictures might have been considered disrespectful. In this culture perhaps this is a big enough mistake that the man truly believed an evil spirit would come to dole out punishment," the voice suggested.

Jasmine finally figured out who her dad was talking to. It must have been that anthropologist he'd mentioned before, the one who he'd hoped could give him more information about the tribe he'd visited.

Her dad sighed. Everyone seemed to be doing a lot of sighing these days. "His anger . . . ," he began. "It was so intense. It was as if it had jumped out of his body and was bouncing all around the carving studio."

"I see," Dr. Wilson said.

"And I'm disappointed in myself for being so inappropriate," her dad added. "I wasn't traveling with a photographer, and the magazine insisted on seeing some photos. But I know better than that, I really do. My photographer, Buddy, would never have let this happen."

"Well, it sounds like you've punished yourself enough, Martin," the voice said with a sympathetic chuckle. "My advice is, write a great piece that teaches your readers about this little-known culture. That is your contribution."

"Thank you, Dr. Wilson," Jasmine's dad said. He sighed once again. "I'll try to do that."

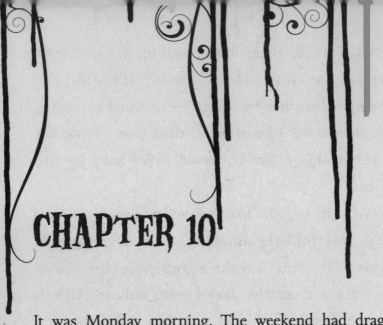

CHAPTER 10

It was Monday morning. The weekend had dragged by. Jasmine and Lisa still hadn't spoken, and Jasmine awoke with a feeling of dread. It was Mini-Course Day, and she remembered she had signed up for Mardi Gras mask-making. And so had Lisa. What terrific timing. Why did she have to choose that as a workshop? *Haven't I had enough of masks for one week?* she thought. *Haven't I had enough of Lisa?*

But the truth was, Jasmine missed Lisa already. She hated being in a fight with her.

As Jasmine entered the classroom, she saw a long table full of craft supplies set up in the middle of the room, so colorful that it looked like a Mardi Gras parade would be starting during Mini-Course Day. There were little pots of paint, jars of paintbrushes and water, glue, beads in all sizes, colored feathers, sequins, glitter, pom-poms, yarn, and ribbons. There were all colors for kids to choose from, but there was a ton of materials in purple, gold, and green.

Some kids were already sitting around the table, waiting for the teacher to come in. Lily and Nina waved at Jasmine. And there was Lisa, an empty seat next to her, a shy smile on her face. She seemed like she hoped Jasmine would come and sit with her. Jasmine took a deep breath and walked toward the seat. She could feel Lisa's relief that she wasn't still totally mad. It was kind of weird. They were making up, but they didn't have to say anything out loud. That was easy.

My problem is that I let my imagination run away with me in the dark, Jasmine thought. *And Lisa's problem is that she thinks it's a big joke. And she doesn't understand how scared I really am. But maybe I can be less of a scaredy-cat. And maybe Lisa will be a little more sensitive now.*

"Good morning, everyone," Mr. Aaronson called as he entered the room. Suddenly Jasmine's life felt like it was turning back to normal. Jasmine had always liked

Mr. Aaronson. Some kids said he had traveled around the world—like, literally, bought an around-the-world plane ticket and stopped in different countries, making a complete circle around the globe. He was also kind of artsy. It made sense that he'd be teaching this mini-course.

"When the teachers were asked about ideas for mini-courses this year, I thought about what I had to offer you guys," he said. "I thought about my trip to Bali, Indonesia, where I learned traditional mask-making. Beautiful masks are used mostly in dance performances there. Well, we won't be making traditional Balinese masks today, but all masks, across cultures, have things in common. Anyone?"

A boy named Logan raised his hand. "They hide you. They're disguises," he said.

"Yes," Mr. Aaronson said. "Disguise is one universal purpose of masks. For this reason, they can be scary, since you never really know for sure who's behind them. And some cultures use them in sacred rituals. But there are other purposes, like entertainment. Like the ones we see at Mardi Gras." He gestured to the board where there were several colorful photos of masked revelers at Mardi Gras.

"Masks play an important role in our understanding of what it means to be human," he continued. "I've always been interested in masks because they allow the wearer to have an experience that really utilizes his or her imagination. By putting on a mask, a person can imagine what it is like to be transformed—changed—into something else."

"Like on Halloween," Logan added.

"Yup," Mr. Aaronson said. "Exactly, Logan. Now, look at this one." He scrolled to another picture. It was of a wooden mask with round eyes. "This is a war mask from the Grebo people of the Ivory Coast and Liberia," he explained.

Another picture. "And here's one from the ancient Aztecs. Believe it or not, the ancient Aztecs prized skulls as war trophies, and skull masks were not uncommon."

Jasmine could feel her classmates shiver at this fact.

Another click. "This is a Noh mask from Japan," he continued, pointing at the photo of a delicate white mask. "These masks are worn during very long performances, so they are very light. There are different types of masks, depending on the character being portrayed."

Mr. Aaronson turned back to look at the class. "Okay. Now *you're* going to be the mask-makers. Everyone, choose a partner. You're going to make quick-drying molds of one another's faces. The material we're using is like papier-mâché, but it's a special kind that hardens in just a few minutes. I got it from a friend who makes monster costumes for movies. You're going to apply a thin layer of this goop to one another's faces. Just pretend you're giving a facial." He laughed at his own joke. "Sit with your partner as the mask dries so they don't freak out. It's kind of a weird feeling to have the goop on your face, and your face will feel tight as the goop dries. When the mask dries, pull it gently off your partner's face. Then you can decorate them with everything you see here." He made a grand, sweeping gesture at the craft supplies.

Jasmine and Lisa looked at each other. There was no question they'd be partners. Lily and Nina sat across the table from them, and they partnered up too. Oh, it was so nice to have everything be back to normal.

"You go first," Jasmine said to Lisa. "I'll do your mask, then you do mine."

"Okay." Lisa nodded.

Jasmine was relieved Lisa had agreed to have her mask done first. The whole thing seemed a little freaky, to be honest. *There I go again,* Jasmine thought. But she walked calmly over to the sink area, where Mr. Aaronson was passing out small bowls of goop for them to smear on one another's faces. It looked like vanilla pudding. She brought it back to the table and placed it in front of Lisa as if she were serving her friend a bowl of delicious dessert. They both laughed.

Jasmine sat down and faced Lisa, and Jasmine began to spread the goop gently on Lisa's face in a thin layer so it covered everything but her eyes, nostrils, and mouth. The goop was cool and slimy. Lisa looked kind of uncomfortable. When Jasmine had covered Lisa's whole face, she said, "Okay, I'm sitting with you right here till it dries. Don't move your face!" Jasmine wiped her hands off on a paper towel. Lisa struggled to stay still, but the mask dried quickly, just like Mr. Aaronson had promised.

"Ready?" Jasmine asked Lisa, her fingers around the edge of Lisa's mask, ready to pull it off. Lisa nodded, and Jasmine gently pulled it away from her skin. And there was Lisa's face—in her hands. So weird! She placed the mask on the table in front of them, and Lisa touched it gently. "Cool," Lisa said. "That's really cool."

"Okay, I guess it's my turn," Jasmine said. Lisa got down to business with the goop.

The goop was cool and slippery-feeling on Jasmine's face, but she felt the warmth of Lisa's fingers in contrast. Lisa spread the goop carefully and evenly over Jasmine's whole face. And before she knew it, Lisa was done. "There," Lisa said, sitting back and smiling proudly. "Now just let it dry."

As Jasmine's mask dried, her face felt weirdly tight. She started to feel a little panicky, but before she knew it, Lisa was carefully removing the mask, pulling it slowly from her face.

Then the two sat there, silently examining the shells of their faces. It was weird to be looking at her face somewhere other than in a mirror or in a photo.

"Let me guess," Jasmine broke the silence. "You're going to make your mask scary, and I'm not, right?" They both laughed. There. All the tension was gone. Jasmine was so relieved they weren't in a fight anymore. She was sure that from now on Lisa would be more aware of how Jasmine just got a little, well, *scared* sometimes.

Jasmine and Lisa walked over to the craft table together to gather materials to decorate their masks.

Jasmine was in a pink mood today so she selected pink everything: pink glitter, pink sequins, pink feathers, pink yarn, pink beads, pink ribbons. She placed everything beside her blank mask, along with a small bottle of glue.

"Are you sure you have enough pink?" Lisa asked, looking over at Jasmine's choices, and they both cracked up.

Lisa picked Mardi Gras colors. As they worked quietly, carefully focused on gluing, Jasmine peeked at Lisa's mask in progress. Lisa was somehow managing to make a mask that looked terrifying, but also like great fun. While the expression on the mask was angry, Lisa added so many sequins that the mask shone like a hundred stars. *Leave that to Lisa!* Jasmine thought.

After a while Mr. Aaronson said, "Okay, everyone, when you're ready, please set your masks on the table to dry, and then start walking around and looking at what your classmates have made. There's some really beautiful work here. I hope you wear your masks, whether it's to the parade or to parties, or hang them up in your bedrooms." Ha! Jasmine knew she wouldn't be doing *that*, but she was still pleased with her work.

As their masks dried, the class watched a short movie on the history of Mardi Gras. Then the mini-course was over. Jasmine headed down the hall toward the next mini-course, mask in hand, her hands still a little sticky with pink paint and pink glitter. It was time to "Learn a Little Japanese."

When Jasmine got home from school, pink mask in hand, she found a note from her dad on the kitchen table:

Jazzy,

Hope you had a good day at school. I bet you made a pretty mask and learned lots of Japanese. I had to leave for the airport earlier than I thought. I'm sorry I didn't get to say good-bye.

Honey, I hope you are not still feeling scared by the mask. Don't worry—it's harmless! And remember, it's supposed to be there to protect you and Nana, so let it do its job! Also, Lisa is welcome to come over whenever

you girls want, but NO MORE SNEAKING
AROUND IN THE BASEMENT AT NIGHT!

Nana is at her card game and will be
home before dinner. I'll be home in just a few
weeks. I'll blow you kisses from Siberia!

Love you,

Daddy

Jasmine left her pink mask on the kitchen table and
headed upstairs. Her walk was half walk, half stomp: she
was annoyed that her dad had left without saying good-
bye. Until, that is, she was halfway up the stairs. She
looked up and saw the mask staring down at her. Her
anger at her father morphed into anger at the mask. *I
can't take it anymore,* she thought. *I hate this thing.*

Jasmine couldn't help herself. She went straight to
the mask—suddenly she felt superbrave—and removed
it from its hook on the wall. Then she headed straight for
the basement, and her dad's workbench in the corner. It
was an old wood table. Tools hung on a rack above. *Dad
is pretty good at fixing and making things when he isn't traipsing
around the world,* Jasmine thought bitterly.

All of a sudden Jasmine felt strongly that the mask had *no right* to be in her house. If something freaked her out, shouldn't her dad have respected that and at least kept it in his office, where she wouldn't have to look at it all the time? Wasn't it bad enough that he was gone so much? Light-headed with a calm, uncharacteristically daring feeling, Jasmine placed the mask on the cement floor of the basement. Then she grabbed her dad's hammer and crouched over the mask. And before Jasmine even knew what she was doing, she was banging the mask with the hammer—hard. Over and over, again and again. It reminded her of when her dad had brought her home a coconut and they had used a hammer to break it open. The coconut—and mask—were harder to break than she'd expected. Both times Jasmine had to beat down with all her might.

When the mask finally split into three pieces with a loud *crack*, Jasmine realized she was sweating and her hair had come out of its loose ponytail.

Well, there's only one place for the mask now, and it's called the garbage can, Jasmine thought. *And if Nana or Dad notices, I'll just tell them that I accidentally knocked the mask off the wall as I walked by with my big backpack. Ha! Accidentally on purpose, that is!*

Jasmine picked up the three pieces of the mask, careful not to give herself a splinter on its now-rough edges. She felt a wave of relief wash over her. Somehow, with the mask in three pieces, it had lost its power to scare her. It wasn't a mask anymore. It was just pieces of wood. It was garbage, and that's exactly where it was going! Jasmine walked up the basement stairs, wood pieces in hand, and into the kitchen, headed straight for the garbage can.

She placed the mask pieces on top and pressed down on them so they smashed the garbage underneath. Then she realized she should cover them up so Nana wouldn't see them. She took a few sheets of paper towels and crumpled them up, placing them carefully on top of the mask pieces so they wouldn't be that noticeable.

Mission accomplished. *Bye-bye, mask! See you never!* Jasmine thought as she grabbed her pink mask and brought it up to her room, laid it on top of her desk, flopped onto her bed, and turned on the television.

CHAPTER 11

By Friday, Jasmine had almost totally forgotten all about the mask. *Outta sight, outta mind,* she figured. Whenever she passed the empty nail in the hallway above the stairs, she thought about hanging up the pink mask she'd made on Mini-Course Day.

After school Jasmine and Lisa were on Jasmine's living room couch watching a movie. It was gray and raining outside, and Jasmine pulled a plaid blanket that her dad had brought from Scotland over her knees. She felt a nap coming on, actually. Momo was curled up in the crook of her knees, purring so loudly that it was almost distracting. Momo was also doing the hilarious part of his grooming ritual, in which he licked and bit his claws to get the old outer layer off. It was funny to see a cat biting its fingernails. Sometimes Jasmine bit her fingernails when she was nervous, but judging by his happy purring, Momo wasn't feeling nervous in the slightest.

"Are you *asleep*?" Lisa exclaimed, incredulous.

"No," Jasmine said. Before she could defend herself, the doorbell rang. *Dingdong!*

That was odd. Jasmine wasn't expecting anyone and as far as she knew, her grandmother wasn't either. Nana was taking a nap in her room, and she hadn't let Jasmine know of any visitors who might be stopping by. And Jasmine wasn't supposed to open the door for strangers, so she didn't answer. But then the doorbell rang again. Jasmine and Lisa looked at each other.

"Maybe someone just left a package at the door," Jasmine thought aloud.

"You should go bring it in now," Lisa said. "Because of the rain."

"Well, the porch is covered," Jasmine said lazily, letting her eyes close again. "So it won't get wet."

"Well, it's damp out there, and it could still get ruined," Lisa reasoned. "Anyway, if it's a package, don't you want to find out what it is? Maybe it's a present for you. Maybe your dad sent you something from Siberia!"

"Ha." Jasmine laughed. "I don't think so. He said that where he's staying is so remote that you can only get there by helicopter, boat, or dogsled! You're right, though, I'll go bring it in," Jasmine said, groaning, as she threw the blanket back and dragged herself off the couch.

As she approached the front door, the rain sounded even louder. It was quite dark out even though it was only around four o'clock, and the wind was howling. Jasmine looked through the peephole. There was no one there, but there was a package on the porch. She also saw a delivery van driving away.

Jasmine unlocked the door and opened it. The wind was blowing sideways, and raindrops splashed her face. She saw the package on the stairs and ran out to get it quickly before she got soaked.

She barely looked at the package before she dashed back inside. But as Jasmine brought it into the living room, she glanced down and saw her name and address written in a shaky handwriting that she did not recognize. So it was for her, but what could it be?

Lisa had been right: the package was quite damp. It

felt cold, too. It made Jasmine want to crawl back under the plaid blanket.

The package was wrapped in brown paper, like an old grocery bag that had been reused many times, and tied up like a present with twine. She wasn't used to packages arriving like this. Usually they were sturdy brown boxes covered with clear tape, and certainly not tied up with some weird string. She untied the twine and pulled off the paper.

And there, staring back at her through its empty eyeholes, was the last thing she expected to see. The mask.

It was back in one piece, not three. You could still see the cracks, though the pieces had been carefully glued together, and if you didn't know the mask was once broken, you might not even notice them.

"Hey, it's the mask," Lisa said, looking over casually, as if Jasmine wouldn't have known this without Lisa's official announcement! "Why did it come in the mail?"

"I don't know," Jasmine said.

"Wasn't it on the wall?" Lisa asked.

"Yeah, it was," Jasmine said. She hadn't told Lisa about how she had smashed it.

"So why did it come in the mail?" Lisa pressed.

"I don't know," Jasmine said.

"I don't get it," Lisa said again. "Who sent it?"

"No, you really *don't* get it, do you?" Jasmine said. The panic she felt made her voice rise. "I'm *telling* you I don't *know*."

"Okay," Lisa mumbled, her voice low. Then she seemed to remember how scared Jasmine must have been feeling. She knew the mask was a problem for her, after all. It had certainly been a problem in their friendship over the weekend. "Sorry," she said quickly. "That's just really weird that it came in the mail. Like, all of a sudden."

Jasmine said nothing. She just stared openmouthed at the mask.

Then a sound somewhere between a *crash*, *bang*, and *zap* reverberated through the house. A bolt of lightning struck a tree in the front yard. Electric white-blue light filled the living room, like no light Jasmine and Lisa had ever seen.

Spectral was what it was. That had been on a recent vocabulary list of Jasmine and Lisa's. It meant ghostly.

Startled, Jasmine dropped the mask. It fell onto the

hardwood floor with a loud clatter. The sound was loud enough to scare Momo, who, already on edge from the lightning, bristled. He arched his back and ran out of the room in a flash.

Then *boom, boom, boom!* went the loudest thunder Jasmine and Lisa had ever heard. Barely a second had passed between the lightning and thunder, so they knew the storm was really close. They both screamed. And screamed and screamed. So loudly that Jasmine covered her own ears to drown out the sound.

CHAPTER 12

Nana came rushing into the living room. Jasmine couldn't help it; she ran over to her and threw her arms around her. The last time Jasmine had done that, she had reached only Nana's knees.

Jasmine and Lisa were both freaked out. Truly. Freaked. Out.

Nana looked at the mask on the floor. "Oh, honeybunch, Nana thought you'd be happy," Nana said to Jasmine. That was one really weird thing about Nana. She sometimes talked about herself in the third person, like *Give Nana a hug* or *Nana loves Jasmine.*

"Happy?" Jasmine looked at Nana in disbelief. How could Nana think she'd be happy?

"Well," Nana continued, "I know you tried to get rid of this mask. I'm not sure how it got broken, but I don't need to know that. And I don't know why you're so scared of it, but I know that you put it in the garbage. And I didn't want you to get in trouble for it. Also, Nana didn't want you to hurt your dad's feelings. He puts a lot of thought into the gifts he brings back for us, you know."

Jasmine just stared at Nana. Was she trying to make her feel guilty?

"So Nana sent it out to be fixed," Nana continued, patting Jasmine's back like she did when she was little. "I wanted to surprise you with it. That's why I had the repair person address the package to you."

"Well, you sure surprised me!" Jasmine said, groaning. Clearly, she was never going to be able to get rid of this thing. She felt deeply resigned that the mask was here to stay. Ugh. What was she going to do?

Jasmine signed dramatically. "Could we at least not hang it up again?" she asked Nana. "Or even better, could it just not be in the house, so I don't have to look at it all the time? I don't care where. I just don't want to see it."

"Sure, honeybunch," Nana said soothingly. "Why don't you hide it wherever you want? You don't even have to tell me where it is. Just don't throw it away, because it would hurt your dad's feelings. But wait. Nana wants to tell you girls something. I want to teach you some tricks to get rid of your fear."

Jasmine groaned and laughed at the same time. "Ready for the superstitions?" she asked Lisa. They grinned at each other.

"Okay," Nana said. "To banish fear, here's what you do. Snap your fingers five times next to each ear and say, 'Be gone, fear!'"

If only it were that easy, Jasmine thought. *Nana has no idea.*

"And here's another thing you can try," Nana said. She really was trying to be helpful, Jasmine knew, so she listened quietly. "Sleep with a bar of soap under your pillow. It will wash the fear out of your mind while you sleep."

But as Nana looked at Jasmine, she realized nothing she was saying was helping. She looked sympathetic. "What would make you feel better right now, Jasmine?" she asked kindly.

Jasmine knew right away. There *was* one thing that would truly help. "Can Lisa spend the night tonight, Nana?" Jasmine asked. She had a feeling Nana would say yes.

"Of course. If Lisa's parents say it's okay," Nana said right away. "And, if you two like, I can make my famous dumpling soup." She usually made this on Sundays. Nana always put a dried apricot inside one of the dumplings. If you got the apricot in one of your dumplings, that was supposed to mean you'd have good luck for a week.

But the truth was that Jasmine just didn't want any more surprises—in a dumpling or anywhere else.

"That's okay, Nana," Jasmine said. "Thanks, but I'm not really in the mood for dumpling soup."

"No problem," Nana said. "How about if I make a fire? It sure is the perfect night for it." She started putting logs into the fireplace. Now *that* sounded like a good idea to Jasmine. It was so nice to sit in front of the fire. Momo usually joined her, and tonight it would be her and Lisa, all warm and cozy.

"Thanks, Nana," Jasmine said. She really was starting to feel a little bit better. "Come on," she said to Lisa, taking the two blankets and cushions off the couch. "Come sit in front of the fire." Nana got the fire started quickly as the storm continued to whistle and wail outside. Then Nana left the girls alone again and went to fix dinner.

"Well, then," Jasmine said to Lisa. "Enough excitement for you?" She was being sarcastic, but she saw on Lisa's face that she had actually been really freaked out as well. Jasmine had to admit: it made her feel a little better that Lisa got scared sometimes too.

"Seriously, though," Lisa said. Her face matched the word perfectly. "Why are you so petrified of that mask?"

Jasmine sighed loudly. "You really want to know?"

"Of course," Lisa answered. Her face showed the excitement that she usually showed when talking about ghosts, but this time Jasmine thought she detected some nervousness in her expression too.

"I hated the mask the first time I saw it," Jasmine admitted to her best friend. "It creeped me out, and now I've even had nightmares about it."

Lisa nodded sympathetically. Jasmine finally felt that Lisa got it.

"And then you did that horrible thing of scaring me in the basement," Jasmine had to add. They hadn't discussed it since the morning after it had happened.

"I'm really sorry," Lisa said quickly. "I was trying to be funny. But I totally get how it backfired."

Jasmine smiled as she stared at the fire. It was mesmerizing to watch the flames. She imagined tossing the mask right into them and watching it burn.

"But you're right about that mask," Lisa went on. "It *is* creepy. So what happened? You broke it, then you threw it away?"

"Yeah," Jasmine confessed. "I smashed it with a hammer in the basement. *Really* hard!"

Lisa looked impressed, and Jasmine felt strangely proud of herself. She remembered how good the hammer had felt in her hand as she brought it down on the wood again and again with all her might.

"Then I put it in the garbage and covered it up with paper towels," Jasmine said. "I thought it would be gone forever. But as you have seen, I will never be rid of it!" She gave a sad little laugh.

"Well, at least once you hide it, you don't have to look at it anymore," Lisa said. She was trying to say something helpful, Jasmine knew. But all Jasmine could think of was where she could hide that mask. It *had* to be somewhere outside of the house.

"Look, Jas," Lisa said. "There's really nothing to be afraid of. Even if the mask did have special powers, they're supposed to be good ones, right?" But something in her voice let Jasmine know that she was trying to convince herself of this "fact" too.

"You know what?" Jasmine said. She didn't want to answer Lisa's question. "I want to hide that mask right now like Nana said I could. I don't want to wait one minute longer."

"Okay," Lisa said patiently. "I'll help you, but where should we hide it?"

They both thought about it.

And once Jasmine got the idea, she knew it was a good one. "The tree house," she said.

"Wow, I almost forgot about your tree house," Lisa said. "We haven't hung out there in forever. We used to hang out in there all the time, remember?"

Jasmine's dad had built the tree house when she was a little girl. She'd "helped" him by handing him nails, which at the time seemed like an important job, but now she realized her dad had just been trying to make her feel helpful and involved. She'd loved the tree house as a child, spending lots of time there by herself reading or hanging out with Lisa and other friends. They'd pretend they were grown-ups, and that it was their actual house. But as Jasmine got older, she'd stopped going into the tree house as much. In the past year she hadn't gone inside at all. So it was the perfect place to hide something she never wanted to see again.

"Yeah," Jasmine said. She looked outside. The storm had stopped, and the sun was starting to shine for the last few minutes of daylight. She already had her shoes on, and the mask in her hand, ready to go. She couldn't get it out of the house fast enough!

Lisa put her shoes on quickly too, sensing how important this mission was to Jasmine. Jasmine opened the back door.

The girls ran across the yard and climbed carefully up the wooden ladder, which was not easy for Jasmine to do while holding the mask with one hand. But as soon as they entered the tree house, which had a very good roof, they sat down and breathed a sigh of relief. Jasmine felt better already. They looked around. Everything was exactly as they remembered it. There were still four plastic chairs in there, and a wooden table her dad had built. There were still a few posters of animals on the walls.

They were a little weathered. But it really was a great tree house. And Jasmine appreciated it more than she ever had before, because it was going to be the mask's new home. Now it could protect the squirrels and the birds and leave Jasmine alone!

Jasmine and Lisa sat on the chairs, catching their breaths. Jasmine put the mask down, and it sat on the floor between them.

"You know what? Let's get out of here," Jasmine said. "It's cold, and I want to get back in front of the fire and warm up. And leave this creepy thing here, of course."

Lisa smiled and stood up, then stepped carefully down the ladder. And Jasmine followed her, leaving that mask where it belonged.

Jasmine and Lisa kicked off their wet, muddy shoes and got right back under their blankets in front of the fire. It was just as cozy as it had been five minutes before. Jasmine felt relief that the mask was no longer in the house, but as the minutes ticked by, she felt herself getting annoyed about the mask. She was no longer as freaked out, just mad.

"What's the matter?" Lisa asked.

"The totally annoying thing about the mask is my dad," Jasmine said. "He brought it back from his trip like it was some wonderful gift. Whenever he brings me back a present, I feel like he's trying to make up for never being around. Like, he just gets to go off and do whatever he wants, and if he brings me back a really cool present, everything's okay. Well, it's not."

The familiar anger filled Jasmine's chest. She took a deep breath. She was getting all worked up again. "Okay. New subject, please!" She forced herself to laugh. "Like, what are we doing for the Mardi Gras parade?" It was coming up that weekend, and they usually went together.

"Well, we're definitely wearing the masks we made," Lisa answered.

"Stop saying *masks*!" Jasmine sincerely meant it, but they both laughed.

"Sorry," Lisa said quickly. "Well, you know how Jordan lives on the parade route, and she's going to have her party again this year?"

Jasmine knew that. Jordan had invited her, she remembered, but with everything going on, she'd completely forgotten about it. She remembered how much fun Jordan's party had been last year. About ten kids had been invited. They had stood on the second-floor balcony and watched the crazy parade go by. The bright colors, the outrageous costumes, the inventive floats—they were unbelievable. All the kids wore tons of purple, gold, and green beads. They also painted one another's faces with purple, gold, and green face paint, and ate so much king cake that Jasmine thought she would explode.

Of course, lots of marchers in the parade wore masks. Remembering how colorful and fun all the masks were, Jasmine had a moment of envy of all the partiers' clueless fun. *Imagine if they had a real mask to deal with!* she thought.

But her thoughts were interrupted by Nana approaching them with a smile and two plates—a fireside dinner. What a special treat.

"Thanks, Nana," Jasmine said as she reached up and took her plate. Lasagna!

"Thanks, Nana," Lisa said too as Nana handed her a plate. *It's sweet how Lisa calls her Nana too,* Jasmine thought. It made Jasmine feel like they were all family.

"The storm passed by so quickly. One minute there was thunder and lightning, and now the sky is clear as a bell," Nana said as Jasmine stuck her fork into the lasagna and lifted the first bite high off her plate, the cheese stretching about two feet long. They all laughed.

"Works for me," Lisa said. "I really don't like thunder and lightning."

Jasmine felt sort of good hearing that Lisa didn't like storms. *I guess everyone is afraid of something,* she thought.

Jasmine was pleasantly surprised. It had turned out to be kind of a great night. The mask felt faraway in the tree house. Soon after they filled their bellies with lasagna, Jasmine and Lisa fell sound asleep, curled up on the rug right in front of the fire. Just like happy cats.

But the wind rattling the window next to the fireplace woke up Jasmine soon after. She looked over at Lisa, who was fast asleep, the dimming, flickering firelight giving her face a pretty orange glow.

It's just the wind, Jasmine had to remind herself. She looked at the flames in the fireplace. They were always soothing. Maybe they would calm her down.

But then . . . *Rattle, rattle, rattle.* The sound just would not stop, and it was so loud that Jasmine knew she would have trouble going back to sleep. *You're okay. You're okay. You're okay*, she said to herself.

Her eyes moved to the rattling window.

And there it was.

The mask! That wooden face! As if it were a person outside in the damp, cold night, looking in.

And even though the mask had just holes for eyes, it looked to Jasmine as if the eyes were looking straight into her soul.

CHAPTER 13

Jasmine sat straight up. The tall grandfather clock next to the couch said it was 4:25. It was the third time in a row that she'd woken up from a nightmare at that exact same time.

I can't take this anymore, Jasmine thought. She put her face in her hands. *I can't take these nightmares.* It felt like her brain was rattling around in her skull, trying to find a way out of her head.

But it wasn't her brain that was rattling. It was the window, just like in her nightmare. Jasmine looked around and wrapped her arms around herself in a big hug to check that she was really in her body. To check that this wasn't still part of the nightmare. It wasn't, she was sure of it. Again, she looked over at Lisa. And again, Lisa was peacefully asleep.

You're okay. You're okay. You're okay. Jasmine kept her eyes on the fire to calm herself down. The flames were as short as her fingers, and tiny embers glowed at the bottom like baby fireflies. Jasmine took a deep breath. She listened carefully for the rattling sound but didn't hear it anymore. She just heard the sound of glass breaking, as if someone had dropped a mug on a hard floor.

And then. *Whoosh. Buzz. Screech. Whoosh! Buzz! Screech!*

All Jasmine knew was that something was buzzing and flapping so loudly that it seemed like there was nothing else in the whole world except those noises. She screamed. It sounded to her like her scream was coming from someone else. It was super-high-pitched, nothing at all like any noise she had ever made, not even when Lisa had scared her in the basement and not even when the mask had been delivered to her door earlier that day. Lisa woke up with a jolt and immediately joined Jasmine in screaming, not even knowing why.

For the second time that evening, Nana ran into the room looking alarmed. But this time the girls did not stop screaming. They kept their eyes closed and their hands over their ears, as if to block out the world. They pulled their blankets over their heads.

And it was a good thing they did. An unrecognizable and very large insect was flying frantically around the room *screeching* as Jasmine and Lisa both huddled and cowered, crying, under their blankets.

The screen must have been open a bit, and the insect had gotten stuck between the screen and the pane. That was what the rattling had been all about. The insect had been beating itself against the window, trying to escape, and had eventually broken the pane—that was the sound of breaking glass Jasmine had heard—and flown right into the room.

The bug landed on the coffee table in front of the couch. The room was silent; there was no more screeching or buzzing or whooshing. Jasmine and Lisa somehow gathered the courage to peek out from under the covers. Nana had closed the screen and turned on the overhead light. Jasmine couldn't believe what she saw.

The horrifying insect had a red body and wings like a moth, but they were enormous—each one the size of a sheet of notebook paper. Its body, the size of a banana, was red and hard. It looked like it would crunch loudly if you stepped on it, which Jasmine really wanted to do, even though it would probably be disgusting. She raised her foot bravely, ready to stomp, then realized she was barefoot.

"No, honeybunch, we're not going to kill it." Nana stopped Jasmine. "Nana's going to humanely capture it and put it outside where it belongs. Just because we haven't seen any bug like this before, and just because it's big, and okay, I admit, a little scary-looking, doesn't mean we should kill it."

"What does humanely mean?" Lisa asked curiously, as if she were sitting in Ms. Berger's English class. As if this was a perfectly normal moment. Jasmine was still unable to speak.

"Well, what word do you hear in *humane?*" Nana asked Lisa, as if she were a teacher.

"Human!" Lisa exclaimed.

"That's right," Nana said. She seemed pleased that Lisa was following along. "It's human, but with an *e* at the end. You can think of the *e* as standing for 'extra,' like the extra-good qualities of being human. Everything that is excellent about people, like being gentle and treating every living creature with respect, even if it doesn't serve our purposes. Especially if it can't take care of itself. Like this bug here. It's trapped, basically."

Lisa nodded intently. The bug stayed completely still.

"*Hello!*" Jasmine said loudly. "Can the vocabulary lesson please be over until we get this—thing—out of here?" What were they thinking, talking about vocabulary words? Were they for real?

"Hold your horses," Nana said gently. She went into Jasmine's dad's office and quickly came back with a piece of printer paper. "Here," she said. "We'll slide it onto this paper and then put the paper on the porch." The insect remained completely motionless. "Oh, look, the poor thing is scared."

"That *poor thing* tried to kill me!" Jasmine exclaimed.

"Don't be so dramatic," Nana said. "And think of the cats and dogs in the animal shelter. This bug is an animal, just like them. All living things should be treated with respect."

That actually made good sense to Jasmine. Then the insect's buggy, yellow eyes looked right at her. Jasmine and the insect seemed to be locked in a stare. Jasmine thought of the expression "His eyes bugged out of his head." Now she understood it perfectly.

She got a closer look. The insect had sharp, curvy

fangs. Its antennae were long. Too long.

Nana used her foot—luckily, she was wearing slippers—to push the insect onto the paper. Then she carefully picked it up. The weight of the insect made the thin sheet of paper sag. Nana carried it to the back door.

"Open this door for Nana, girls," Nana said. "Unless you want your visitor to spend the night!" She seemed to think this was funny. Jasmine followed Nana and opened the door as quickly as she could. As if it knew it was outside again, the insect flew off the piece of paper. Jasmine couldn't be sure, but it looked like it was headed for the tree house.

After the girls and Nana had finished cleaning up the broken glass, it was time to go back to sleep.

"Let's go upstairs," Jasmine said quickly to Lisa. "We can sleep in my room instead of down here."

"I don't have my sleeping bag," Lisa reminded her.

"You can fit in my bed with me," Jasmine replied.

In Jasmine's room the girls huddled close in the dark. They tried to calm themselves down by staring at the glowing constellations on the ceiling.

"You want to know something?" Lisa finally said. "It turns out that I'm not so into scary things anymore."

"Gee, I can't imagine why," Jasmine said, sighing.

"It used to be kind of fun to get scared, like when you're on a roller coaster," Lisa went on. "But enough is enough. Seriously."

Jasmine couldn't have agreed more. "How are we ever going to get to sleep?" she wondered aloud. They lay in silence.

"I know," Lisa said. "My mom taught me this trick. We'll count backward from one hundred. By the time we get to zero, we'll be asleep."

"Promise?" Jasmine said hopefully.

"Promise," Lisa said.

And thankfully, she was right. They were both asleep by the time Lisa counted down to fifty. All their screaming that afternoon and night had really tired them out.

CHAPTER 14

Jasmine woke up feeling grateful. She hadn't had any more nightmares. She didn't even remember having any dreams. *I guess reality was enough of a nightmare last night,* she thought. *That bug!* Jasmine remembered exactly what it looked like, but she wished she didn't. And she knew she'd never forget the sound that its giant, flapping wings had made. Lisa was still asleep—of course!—but it was time to get up. It was Saturday, but they both had things to do that day. Today was the fund-raiser at the shelter, and Lisa had to go to softball practice. Jasmine lay in bed for a few minutes, her eyes open, preparing for another day. Her eyes rested on the pink mask she'd made, which now hung on her wall. She decided to take it down later that day. She now officially had a bad feeling about masks in general.

In fact, she was convinced that the mask—not the pretty one she'd made, but *the* mask—had something to do with the buggy horror of last night. She didn't understand the logic of how the two things were connected. She just *knew*.

What am I so scared of? Jasmine asked herself. She felt like she needed to approach this whole situation with a little logic. *Okay,* she thought, *what would Dad do? He would "do the research, go to the literature," as he likes to say. Information is power. He gathers as much information as he can. Usually he starts online.*

Jasmine got out of bed, careful to not disturb Lisa. She sat down at her desk and opened her laptop. And as the screen lit up, she closed her eyes and thought of the thing she was most afraid of in the whole world.

She had to be brave and admit the truth to herself. She had to get the information. Only then could she stop being so scared all the time. Only then would her nightmares stop. That was the idea.

The bogeyman.

She typed *bogeyman* into the search bar. She wasn't

even sure how to spell it. But a page came up first thing, and Jasmine clicked on it to find out more. "A legendary ghostlike monster," the page said. Jasmine went on to read that *bogey* was related to the word *bug*.

Jasmine sat back in her chair as a chill went down her spine. This could not be just a coincidence. She'd done the search because she secretly hoped she'd find out how it was all legend . . . all just make-believe children's stories . . . but instead she discovered that the events of last night could really be related to her worst fears.

That bug was announcing something. Jasmine just knew it. Predicting something. It was like a messenger.

A messenger from the bogeyman.

Jasmine made it through her day acting as normal as possible. It helped that she was around animals in the shelter, but she was still very uneasy. After the animal shelter fund-raiser was over, she decided to walk to the nearby university's campus, which was between the shelter and home, and visit the library to see what she could find out about the mask. *Information is power,* she kept reminding herself. *Go to the literature.* She'd had some babysitters who went to the university, and she'd also been there with her dad when he was doing research, so she knew her way around a little. She entered the library—it was so big, with high ceilings—and stopped at the front desk.

"Is it okay if I come in and look at books here? I'm not a student. Well, I'm a student, but not at the university, of course," she explained to the librarian, laughing nervously.

"Of course," the woman behind the counter said. "You can't take any books out, though, unless you're a student or a professor. Can I help you find anything?"

How could Jasmine explain? "Um, do you have an anthropologist section?" she asked. Maybe she could find more information written by anthropologists about the island, the tribe, the mask, the legend—anything was better than not knowing.

"Do you mean anthropology?" the librarian asked kindly.

"Um, yeah," Jasmine said, feeling a little sheepish.

"The anthropology collection is on the third floor, way in the back," the librarian said. She seemed impressed a girl Jasmine's age would be interested in anthropology, even if she didn't really know the word.

Well, I was never interested in anthropology before, because I'd never even heard of it, but now it may be a matter of life or death, Jasmine thought. "Thank you," she said politely.

Once she got into the anthropology room and threw her backpack down on a chair, Jasmine used all the research skills she'd learned in school. And between the computer and all the old books and papers, she found out plenty. More than she'd wanted to know, actually.

She found an old dusty book called *Masks of the World: An Anthropological Perspective*. Each chapter had been written by a different professor about a different culture. As she opened the front cover to the table of contents, the name of the island her dad had visited jumped out at her. She turned right to that chapter. The information seemed to flood her eyes faster than she could read it. It was practically jumping off the page, through her eyeballs and into her brain. She had to close her eyes every once in a while because the experience of reading it was so intense.

"'Members of the tribe believe that the mask protects the house it is displayed in,'" she first read. "'If the owner of the mask senses evil approaching his or her home, he or she can put on the mask and ward off the evil. The mask repels the bad spirit, and prevents any harm from coming to him or her.'"

I already knew that part, Jasmine thought. *Dad told me.*

But Jasmine read on: "'However, tribal legend states that if the mask-maker becomes angry when making the mask or he believes that evil spirits have been aroused before a mask is finished, the power of the mask may shift and change.'"

Jasmine took a deep breath.

And then: "'In that instance, the mask is then believed to take on a sinister quality. It is believed that its magic can become so strong that it attracts forces of evil.'"

Jasmine had to look up the word *sinister*. It meant "threatening evil." There were lots of synonyms. They were all words that Jasmine didn't like, such as *menacing, threatening, frightening, dark,* and *black.*

Yeah, sinister. Like the bogeyman, Jasmine thought.

And then this: "'There have been several vague reports about "unfortunate" things happening to people who hang the mask after its powers have turned, but nothing that can be substantiated. Further study of this aspect of the masks and their makers is needed.'"

Jasmine flashed back to the conversation she had heard her dad have with Dr. Wilson, the anthropologist: *. . . he didn't seem afraid. He was angry. Said that I summoned some evil. . . . It was so intense. It was as if it had jumped out of his body and was bouncing all around the carving studio.*

And just like the pieces of the broken mask had been expertly put back together, Jasmine figured out the whole thing. It all made perfect sense now.

The mask may have originally been meant for protection, but there was no telling what its real powers were now. *Because the mask-maker had become angry when making the mask!* His anger had jumped out of his body, as her father had described. It had bounced around the carving studio. And it had entered the mask. The anger had entered the mask, and its power had changed from protection to the very opposite.

Jasmine closed the book. She felt like her stomach was melting. Because she now knew something her father and Nana did not. She knew that it was entirely possible that she—and her dad and Nana—were doomed.

The mask is a magnet, Jasmine kept thinking. *A horrible magnet of doom. A magnet for the bogeyman!*

Jasmine slammed the book shut and walked quickly out of the library, ignoring the nice librarian, who called out: "Did you find what you were looking for, dear?"

Yes, Jasmine thought. *Yes, I sure did. And I wish I hadn't.* She pushed the heavy library door open and ran out into the bright afternoon sun. She had to squint so that she could even see. She couldn't get out of that library fast enough, far away from that book.

There's no one who understands this crazy problem, she thought. *Dad's in Siberia. Who can I turn to for help?*

And then she remembered. *Dr. Wilson.* The anthropologist. He probably taught at this university. Her dad always went to him with his questions. He could give her advice on what to do, how to protect herself. If there was any advice to give, that was.

Jasmine looked at the big campus map near the entrance to the library and found the anthropology department. It was really close. She took a deep breath and walked toward it. There it was, perfectly easy to find. As she opened the door, she felt resourceful and brave. *Look at me, chasing down information.*

She looked at the directory on the wall of which professors were in which offices. There it was: *James Wilson,*

202. Jasmine ran up one flight of stairs and saw a door with a little nameplate that said JAMES WILSON, PHD, PROFESSOR OF ANTHROPOLOGY. Wow. That was easy. Jasmine took another deep breath and knocked on the door.

"Come on in," a man called out.

Jasmine opened the door slowly. Now she felt like her usual shy self, no longer so brave and resourceful. She poked her head into the doorway just a tiny bit, suddenly aware that she was interrupting this man at work.

"Um, hello . . . ," Jasmine began. Then she had no idea what to say next.

"Hello there," Dr. Wilson said, pushing his chair away from his computer and swiveling to turn toward Jasmine. "How can I help you?"

"Um, my name is Jasmine Porter," Jasmine said.

"Marty Porter's daughter?" Dr. Wilson asked. He seemed really friendly. Jasmine was relieved he already knew who she was.

"Yes." She gave a little smile. "I heard you talking on the phone to him the other day. About the mask."

"Ah, yes," Dr. Wilson said, nodding in recognition. "We discussed the tribe he visited and the mask they gave him. I remember he was feeling badly about the mask-maker being angry with him. So what brings you here?"

"Well . . . ," Jasmine stalled, aware of how crazy this whole thing was going to sound. "I'm having some—I don't know—problems. With the mask. And my dad's in Siberia. So I thought I would come to you for advice on what to do."

Dr. Wilson smiled kindly. "Of course, Jasmine," he said. "Anything. I've known your dad for a long time. Whatever I can do to help."

"Well, the mask has freaked me out since the first time I saw it," Jasmine said. "And now I feel like something else is happening. Something big and weird. I'm getting a really bad feeling about it. I don't know why, or what it is."

"What happened?"

Jasmine shivered with the memory. "Last night—"

But Dr. Wilson interrupted her. "Jasmine, have you seen any kind of bug lately? One you've never seen before?" he asked. He seemed worried about what her answer would be. He seemed like he didn't even want to ask.

Jasmine gulped. "Yes," she said. "This strange huge bug flew into our living room. I'd never seen a bug that looked like this. It reminded me somehow of the mask. It was the same color. That's one of the reasons I'm so freaked out."

Then Dr. Wilson stopped smiling. He didn't take his eyes off Jasmine.

"What happened to the bug?" he asked slowly, in a low voice.

"Um, I don't know," Jasmine said. "What do you mean?"

"Did you *kill* the bug, Jasmine?" Dr. Wilson looked very concerned.

Jasmine remembered her grandmother's speech about doing the humane thing and not killing it. She was suddenly glad that they put it outside, even though she wished it weren't still out there. She thought Dr. Wilson would be impressed by their kind choice.

"No," Jasmine reported proudly. "We did the humane thing and put it outside."

Dr. Wilson was silent. He stared at Jasmine.

When he spoke, his voice was heavy and serious. "I see," he said. Then he looked away, out the window. There was a long silence.

"So what do you think I should do? What's up with

this mask?" Jasmine finally asked. She was shocked by Dr. Wilson's expression. He looked like someone had just told him that an asteroid was headed straight for Earth. At the same time, he seemed to be deep in thought. It was an odd combination.

"When does your dad come home?" he asked.

"Um, in a few weeks," Jasmine answered.

"Can you reach him?"

"No, there's no e-mail where he is. My nana's home, though." Jasmine didn't want Dr. Wilson to think her dad had left her home all by herself.

But suddenly he snapped back into being friendly, nice, and casual. "Well, best not to worry," he said. "After all, it's only a story."

"*What's* only a story?" Jasmine asked.

"What?" Dr. Wilson asked, as if he had no idea what the topic of the conversation had been. As if he had lost track.

"You said, 'It's only a story.' *What's* only a story?"

Dr. Wilson exhaled and carefully folded his hands on his lap. "Nothing," he said a little too brightly. "Never mind. It's nothing at all. I think your imagination is just running away with you."

Another long silence. All Jasmine knew was that she wanted to leave his office immediately. "Okay, thanks, Dr. Wilson," she said quickly. She had to get away from him and that book she'd read in the library. She had to get far away from that horrible information—and from Dr. Wilson's concerned expression.

Jasmine walked down the steps and into the bright light again.

The main thing was, she reminded herself, that the mask was out of the house.

CHAPTER 15

Jasmine managed to eat dinner with Nana without acting like she was freaking out. Once she was in bed, Jasmine did everything she could to not think about what she'd read at the library, the bizarre conversation she'd had with Dr. Wilson, and the look on his face. She counted back from one hundred, like Lisa had taught her. And it worked, thankfully.

But then Jasmine woke up.

She hadn't had a nightmare, as far as she could remember, but she could hear thunder booming overhead. The clock on her night table said 4:25 a.m. Jasmine was getting used to this time of morning. Too used to it. Every roll and rumble of thunder went right through her, as if it were sending vibrations right into her bones.

But wait. Was it thunder? As Jasmine woke up, she began to wonder. It sounded more like drumbeats than thunder.

Jasmine listened harder. No, that sound wasn't drumbeats either. It was hoofbeats, like there was an angry bull just outside her window. Like thunder, but on the ground.

Wake yourself up! Wake yourself up! This is another one of your nightmares! Jasmine said to herself.

But it wasn't; it just wasn't. Jasmine knew. This time, her terror was real.

What if something was coming to get her? Not the bug tonight, but the real bogeyman. The hoofbeats sounded louder and louder, and soon the whole house shook. *There's only one thing I can do to protect myself,* she thought. *I need to wear the mask, like dad and the book said. Who knows if the mask has turned evil or not—all I know is that wearing it is my only hope of defending myself.*

Jasmine knew it would be no use to run into Nana's room for protection. She had to put on that mask, as terrifying an idea as it was.

Jasmine didn't even stop to put shoes on. She ran out the back door in her pajamas, thinking only about the mask's possible power to save her. It was so dark outside. The ground under her bare feet was cold and muddy. Pouring rain soaked her almost immediately, and as she made her way up the tree house ladder, she nearly slipped and fell all the way back down to the ground.

But finally she made it to the top. The wooden door was right in front of her face. She reached out her wet hand to open it. . . .

But it was already slowly opening from the inside.

CHAPTER 16

And when the door opened, Jasmine saw him clearly for the first time. The bogeyman. And he was more terrifying than Jasmine ever could have imagined.

He had the shape of a person, but was scaly as a snake and red as blood. Even in the dark, the red scales practically glowed.

And he was wearing the mask. Even if Jasmine wanted to wear it for protection, it was his now. There was nowhere left for Jasmine to hide.

He just stood there. Jasmine could see his bright yellow eyes through the holes in the mask. They shone like flashlights. They were round and bulging, like the bug's from the night before.

Jasmine fell backward off the ladder and landed on the hard wet grass with a thud, but then she got right up to run away.

But the bogeyman jumped down the ladder in one swift move before Jasmine could get anywhere. He crouched low to the ground.

And then Jasmine felt it. A cold wet grip around her left ankle. A slimy grip, like something between a hand and a claw. And then the bogeyman began to pull, *hard*.

Jasmine dropped her weight and planted her feet in the mud as if she could hold on to it and keep from being dragged away. But the bogeyman was trying to make her fall down. No matter how hard she tried, Jasmine couldn't keep her footing. She lost her balance and fell back into the mud. And the bogeyman's grip around her ankle got even tighter.

Now they were both down in the mud. Jasmine wasn't even thinking. Every ounce of her was just trying to protect herself and get *away*. She scratched and clawed at the bogeyman's face, and as she did so, the mask came off and fell facedown into the mud.

Now Jasmine could see the bogeyman's face. Even in the dark, it was scarier than her worst nightmares.

And the last sensation Jasmine felt was the cold burn of the wet grass on her legs as she was dragged away, through her backyard, through her front yard, down the sidewalk, and far, far away from her home. And the last thing Jasmine heard was her own chanting: "It's just a dream, just a dream, just a dream. You're okay. You're okay. You're okay."

EPILOGUE

TEN YEARS LATER

The family—a mother, father, a boy, and a girl—stood on the front porch of their new house, except it was really an old house, and no one had lived in it for many years. They were talking to the realtor, the woman who had helped them through the process of buying their new home.

The realtor was trying to finish up the conversation so she could get to her next appointment. But she knew she had to give the family one last piece of information; it was the right thing to do. "Oh, did I mention?" she asked the family. "I'm sorry to say you're going to need to clean out the basement yourselves."

"What do you mean?" the mother asked.

"Well, there are some things stored down there," the realtor answered slowly. "Not that much. But no company in town would agree to clean it out, no matter how much we offered. Very strange," she added.

The mother and father nodded patiently. They'd been looking for a house to buy for a long time now, and every house had one problem or another. They supposed this was no worse than any other random issue with a new house, like a leaky roof or a rickety staircase.

"Oh, one more thing," the realtor added. She was already holding her car keys in her hand, getting ready to leave the family in their new home.

"What's that?" the father asked.

"You'll probably want to consult with an expert exterminator," she said casually. "I'm afraid there's been a bit of an ongoing problem with bugs here. I thought we had gotten rid of all of them before we put the house up for sale, but this morning I noticed another one," she added.

The parents looked at each other, their eyebrows raised. The boy and girl looked at them. What was going on?

"You mean an exterminator came but couldn't get rid of the bugs?" the mother asked.

"Yes," the realtor said. "A few different exterminators came, actually. They claimed they had never seen this type of bug before, that it wasn't a bug you usually saw in New Orleans. It's a bit, um, bigger, than your average bug."

The realtor and the family stood in an awkward silence. The boy and girl just looked at their parents.

"Don't worry, guys," the mother said. "Why don't you go explore our new home?"

The kids both ran off.

"Let's check out the basement," the girl said to the boy. They were standing in the kitchen.

"I don't want to get bitten by bugs," the boy said, a note of fear in his voice.

"Come on, scaredy-cat," the girl said. "We have to go down there eventually."

"Okay." The boy sighed.

A very bright fluorescent bulb illuminated their way down the stairs. When they got to the bottom, they looked around. There was a table with tools on it, and boxes stacked neatly against the walls. At the top of one of the stacks of boxes was a piece of carved red wood. It caught the girl's eye.

"Can you reach that?" the girl asked her brother.

"I guess." The boy sighed again, straining to get his hand up that high. He brought the wood down, and the two kids had a coughing fit because of the thick layer of dust that now filled the air. The boy put the piece of wood on a tool table, and more dust rose from it.

The boy and girl stared at it. It wasn't just a piece of wood. It was an old wooden mask, painted deep red, with a beaklike nose and a furrowed brow.

"Cool!" the girl said. She held it right in front of her face and made it dance around a little, wiggling her hips. "I'm gonna show this to Mom and Dad. Maybe we can keep it. Hang it up somewhere. Our first decoration in our new house."

"I don't know," the boy said, covering his eyes with his hands. "It kinda creeps me out."

And that was when the boy's eyes caught some movement in the nearest corner. He crouched down to get a better look. He wasn't entirely sure, but it looked like a red bug with a body as big as a banana and wings as large as notebook paper was staring right back at him.

DO NOT FEAR—
WE HAVE ANOTHER CREEPY TALE FOR YOU!

TURN THE PAGE FOR A SNEAK PEEK AT

You're invited to a

CREEPOVER®

Will You Be My Friend?

"Mom, where does this go?" shouted twelve-year-old Beth Picard. She gripped a large cardboard box in her arms and stood inside the empty hallway of her new house.

"What's it say on the top?" Beth's mom called back from the living room.

Beth glanced down at the box. "'Kitchen,'" she replied.

"I'll give you three guesses as to which room it belongs in," Beth's mom replied. "And the first two don't count!"

"Very funny, Mom," Beth said as she headed to the kitchen and placed the box on top of two other boxes, forming yet another cardboard tower growing out of the kitchen floor.

Beth and her mom were excited about moving into their new house. It had been built a few years ago and had only one set of previous owners. Even the paint on the walls still looked spotless. It felt like a fresh start for both of them.

Beth's mom had just started a new job. Beth was looking to make new friends and move on with her life, following . . . well, following whatever had come before—something she was not too clear about.

Beth hurried back out to the moving truck they had rented, climbed up the metal ramp, and grabbed another box. As she headed down the long front walkway, past hedges and flowering trees, she was about to call to her mom again. Instead she stopped just outside the front door and glanced down at the label on the top of the box. It said BETH'S BEDROOM.

Beth smiled as she walked into the house and headed up the stairs, proud of herself that she didn't have to ask her mom about every box she carried in.

Beth knew that her mom was a very organized person. At least that's what her mom liked to say about herself. She had told Beth that when she packed up their stuff at their old house, she made sure to group every box according to room. Then she made a label for each box to take the guesswork out of the unpacking process.

Beth took her mother's word for the fact that she was organized. In fact Beth took her mom's word for just about everything. For reasons she didn't understand, Beth had trouble recalling the past. She searched her mind, trying to remember helping her mom pack up their old house, but could conjure no images of that or anything else from before. Beth couldn't even recall what their old house looked like.

More to wonder about, I guess, she thought as she stepped into her new bedroom and placed the box onto her bed.

Turning around, Beth caught a glimpse of herself in a full-length mirror leaning against a bedroom wall. Sunlight streaming through the window highlighted the spattering of freckles on her face. She shook her head, sending her shoulder-length auburn hair whipping back and forth.

As Beth was about to turn away and head back downstairs to grab another box, she caught another glimpse of herself in the mirror. In the glass she saw her reflection looking into another mirror, in which she saw herself looking into yet another mirror, and on and on, as if she were in a carnival fun house.

What? she thought, peering into the mirror at the multiple versions of herself. She leaned in closer and saw all the images of herself in the many mirrors lean in as well. She shook her hair again, and strands of copper-colored waves flowed back and forth in each mirror image.

Beth turned away and glanced back quickly, as if she was trying to catch herself, or trying to trick the mirror into going back to normal. Her mirror was still filled with multiple, endless images of herself, extending off into infinity.

Deep into the mirror, way off in the reflected distance, Beth could see the tiniest image. But it wasn't an image of Beth, and it wasn't moving as Beth moved. It was of someone in a long white coat. The woman appeared nervous, looking back over her shoulder again and again. Beth leaned in even closer to the mirror, so that her nose was touching the glass. And that's when the woman vanished from the reflection.

Beth had had enough. She didn't know if she was hallucinating or what, but it was time to get more boxes.

When she turned away from the mirror, all of the other Beths turned with her—all except one who stood still, staring straight out. Beth squeezed her eyes shut tightly, then threw them open quickly. The multiple images were finally gone. The single reflection of Beth, staring wide-eyed at herself in her bedroom was all that remained.

She drew a deep breath and sighed.

"Beth!" her mother called up from the bottom of the stairs. "There's someone here to see you, honey."

I need some sleep, Beth thought, turning away and heading out of her room. Just before she stepped out into the hallway, she whipped around quickly to make sure again that only one image filled the mirror. It did.

A few moments later Beth came face-to-face with a girl her age, standing on the front steps.

"Hi, I'm Chrissy Walters," said the girl. "I'm your neighbor. I just stopped by to welcome you to the neighborhood."

Beth smiled and said hi back.

Chrissy had short blond hair and two different-colored eyes—one blue and one hazel. Beth thought that was totally cool.

"I'm Beth Picard," said Beth. "And this is my mom."

"Nice to meet you," said Chrissy. "I've lived in the house next door for about six months. Your place has been empty all that time. I'm so glad you moved in, especially because we're the same age, I think."

"I just turned twelve yesterday," said Beth.

"Happy birthday!" said Chrissy. "I turned twelve a few weeks ago."

"Come into the kitchen, Chrissy," said Beth's mom. "We can't offer you anything but a glass of water, but you're welcome to sit on a packing crate."

Beth, Beth's mom, and Chrissy all headed down the hall and into the large kitchen, where they found stacks of boxes, a few packing crates, and two glasses sitting on the counter.

"We haven't started unpacking yet," explained Beth's mom. "Just a glass for Beth and a glass for me. Here, let me get you one." She popped open a cardboard box and unwrapped a water glass, then she filled all three glasses with water from the faucet.

"So you only moved into your house recently?" Beth asked Chrissy.

"Yeah, I know a few kids at school, but it's nice to meet someone who lives just next door," said Chrissy.

"Where did you live before this?" Beth asked.

"California," replied Chrissy. "My mom's job moves us around a lot. How about you? Where did you live before this?"

"We lived . . . uh, we lived . . ." Beth stammered and then stopped short. She hit another brick wall in her memory. Try as she might, she could not come up with the name of the town she and her mom had just moved from.

"Rockport." Nancy jumped in. "About an hour from here. On the other side of the city."

"Oh, yeah, Rockport," Beth agreed, although the name of the town meant nothing to her.

"Did you forget where you're from?" Chrissy asked, tilting her head curiously.

"Beth was in an accident a few months ago, Chrissy," Nancy explained. "Sometimes her memory is a bit fuzzy. But the doctors assured us that it will clear up with time. Right, honey?"

"Right," agreed Beth. "That's it. My accident." Though, in truth, Beth had no memory of having had an accident or seeing any doctors.

Beth's mom smiled at her and got up.

"Well, I'll leave you two girls to get to know each other better," Nancy said. "I've got about a million boxes still to unpack. Nice to meet you, Chrissy."

"Nice to meet you, too, Ms. Picard," said Chrissy.

"So maybe we'll be in the same class at school," said Chrissy when Beth's mom had left the kitchen. "That would be fun."

"Actually, my mom is going to homeschool me," Beth explained. "She works the night shift doing medical research at the lab a few blocks from here four nights a week, but she teaches me before she leaves every evening.

"Oh," said Chrissy, unable to disguise the disappointment in her voice.

"But we could hang out together every day when you get home from school and on weekends," Beth added quickly.

Chrissy smiled. "That's great! So what kinda stuff do you like to do? I love reading, playing soccer, and watching movies."

"I like, um, all that stuff too!" Beth replied, not quite sure what she liked to do.

"But you must spend a lot of time alone," Chrissy

added. "Especially at night, with your mom working and all. Is she okay leaving you alone?"

"Actually, there's going to be a babysitter who stays here every night," Beth explained.

"Is she cool?" Chrissy asked.

"I don't know yet," said Beth. "My mom has to find someone now that we've moved. It's a little immature, I know, to have a babysitter at our age, but since my mom works overnight, she doesn't want me home alone all the time."

"That makes total sense," said Chrissy. "I just hope your babysitter is cool, for your sake."

"I'm sure she will be," said Beth. "My mom said I can help her choose the right babysitter. Anyway, I'm really glad you want to be my friend, Chrissy."

"Me too," said Chrissy. "I gotta get home now. But maybe we can hang out tomorrow."

"Great," said Beth.

Both girls headed outside.

"Bye!" said Beth, waving as Chrissy headed to her house.

Beth's mom stuck her head out the front door.

"She seems like a very nice girl," she said. "And it

makes me happy that you'll have a friend close to home. Now, young lady, back to the boxes!"

Beth climbed into the moving truck and picked up another box. She started not to mind so much that she had trouble remembering the past. Here she was in a nice new house, with her mom, and she'd already made a new friend.

Beth Picard was not thinking about the past. She had her sights set squarely on the future.

ALMOST ONE YEAR LATER . . .

Beth raced down the hall, pausing every few seconds to look back over her shoulder.

She's still after me, Beth thought, picking up her pace.

It didn't make logical sense, but the faster Beth ran, the closer the girl in the mirror at the end of the hallway came toward her. And everywhere Beth turned, the mirror and the girl in it followed. Beth stopped short, but the girl in the mirror kept running, getting closer and closer. Spinning back around, Beth found herself staring into a blank wall, as if the hallway she had just come down had vanished.

Who is she . . . and why is she following me?

A door suddenly appeared on her right. She yanked it open and sped through the doorway, slamming it behind her. Beth breathed a sigh of relief. But when she eyed the room she had just stepped into, she was faced with mirrors on every wall. Even the ceiling was totally covered in mirrors jutting out at every angle.

And in each mirror she saw the girl. She knew the girl. That much was certain. But how? From where? Who was she?

Suddenly, impossibly, one of the images of the girl popped out of a mirror in the ceiling and dropped feet first to floor in front of Beth. From this close, she recognized the girl. She looked exactly like her.

What is going on?

The girl said nothing but stared at Beth with a puzzled look on her face. Then she reached out suddenly, grabbed Beth's arm, and said, "You're coming with me!"

"Nooo!" Beth screamed.

When she stopped screaming, Beth realized that she was awake in her bed with her eyes wide open.

It was just another dream, she thought, as her heart pounded away in her chest. *Why do I keep having them?*

Rubbing her eyes and trying to shake the bad dream

from her head, Beth climbed from her bed and walked to the bathroom. She had woken up only a few minutes before her alarm was about to go off. Soon it would be time to begin her daily homeschool lessons with her mom.

Bad dreams aside, Beth was happy in her new life. In the year that had passed since she and her mom had moved into their house, Beth had become comfortable with her daily routine: school lessons in the morning, hanging out with Chrissy in the afternoon, homework in the evenings, and then bed when her mom went to work and Joan, the overnight babysitter, arrived. Life was pretty good.

Especially because Beth and Chrissy had become great friends.

But the best part of the past year was the fact that Beth's memory problems seemed to have disappeared. She still couldn't conjure up memories from before the move, but she tried not to dwell on that, especially because everything that had happened to her during the past year, down to the tiniest detail, remained sharp in her mind.

She could remember the shapes of the snowflakes

during the first snowfall at her new house and building a snowman with Chrissy. She remembered the day they painted her bedroom a shiny purple and the day she decided she hated it and then repainted it lime green.

After breakfast that morning Beth and her mom settled down at the dining room table, books spread across its gleaming oak surface.

"Ok, let's go back to the chapter on Native American history," said Beth's mom, flipping open her book. "I think we left off with the evolution of the Cherokee Nation."

"Yup," said Beth. "Right here in chapter five, the 'Principal Chiefs of the Cherokee Nation.'"

"What can you tell me about the leaders of the Cherokee Nation East?" Beth's mom asked.

"Chief Black Fox was the first great leader of the Cherokee Nation East in the early 1800s," Beth reported. "He was one of the signers of the Holston Treaty and led the tribe for a decade."

"Excellent," her mom said.

Beth grinned proudly. Native American history was a topic that she really enjoyed.

"Let's move on to the Lakota," said her mother, but Beth made no move to turn the page. "Beth, are you okay?"

"What?" Beth replied absentmindedly.

"Am I boring you?" her mom asked, sarcastically. "You're usually very interested in history."

"What? Oh, I'm sorry, Mom. I just had a thought that took me away for a minute. It's funny, but I know more about the history of people who lived hundreds of years ago than I do about my own history."

Beth's mom squirmed a bit in her seat. "But your memory has gotten so much better," she said, unable to disguise the disappointment in her voice.

Beth felt bad, hearing her mother sound upset. She knew her mother wanted nothing more than for Beth to be happy, and she was. She just couldn't help but wonder about her past. She also wondered if her missing memories would haunt her for the rest of her life.

"You're right," she told her mom. "It has, as far as remembering the events since we've been here. But it still feels weird not to remember anything before that."

"I know, honey," Mom said, her tone now much more sympathetic. "That accident robbed you of a lot.

But think of all you have now. A nice home. A good friend."

"Absolutely," Beth said, smiling. "Okay, no more feeling sorry for myself. Back to history."

WANT MORE CREEPINESS?

Then you're in luck, because P. J. Night has some more scares for you and your friends!

HAUNTED WORD SEARCH

As Jasmine learns in this story, people can hide behind masks, both real ones and metaphorical ones. Thirty words or phrases are hidden in this word search below. Can you find them all? Words can appear up, down, backward, forward, or diagonally.

ANTHROPOLOGY	JAZZ	NIGHT-LIGHT
BASEMENT	LIBRARY	NIGHTMARE
BOGEYMAN	LISA	PARADE
DAD	MARDI GRAS	PHOTOGRAPH
EVIL	MASK	POEM
GIFT	METAPHOR	SCAREDY CAT
GUILE	MOMO	TERROR
HAUNTED	MYRIAD	TRAVEL
JAMBALAYA	NANA	TREE HOUSE
JASMINE	NEW ORLEANS	WRITER

READY TO SOLVE?
WE DARE YOU!

```
N A B K I S E D B A S E M E N T J J X G
E T T A B R T J Q U G H A T L T V U P Y
W V F S S V U C A F M S R U K I F X H Q
O S I I A P T R K Z R G D A D H P W P E
R W G L W B O L W H Z F I F V S D S A H
L X R H A H C E B O S R G U I L E C R F
E E K S Z O M O M D E N R E O G O A G I
A U J I Y W K F V L E V A R T N L R O E
N A N A O L Q X J K Z I S R O R R E T J
S N J G N P A R A D E R Q M V O T D O P
J T A Y W R I T E R M H D I H D B Y H N
A H S U E Q V D E T N U A H X P O C P I
M R M A S K J P P L I B R A R Y G A G G
B O I I D B Y C C L G Y J M F C E T G H
A P N C R Q M A E K H O D Y Y I Y F H T
L O E X Z A Z D Y D T C K R L Z M M N L
A L V R O H P A T E M P J I L Z A G I I
Y O L G I F T C B J A X N A N U N E Z G
A G W B W Q M A C N R O O D L O A P N H
A Y K M A B M T R E E H O U S E M B N T
```

Did you find all thirty words?
Check the answer key at the end of the book.

YOU'RE INVITED TO . . .
CREATE YOUR OWN SCARY STORY!

Do you want to turn your sleepover into a creepover? Telling a spooky story is a great way to set the mood. P. J. Night has written a few sentences to get you started. Fill in the rest of the story, and have fun scaring your friends.

You can also collaborate with your friends on this story by taking turns. Have everyone at your sleepover sit in a circle. Pick one person to start. She will add a sentence or two to the story, cover what she wrote with a piece of paper (leaving only the last word or phrase visible), and then pass the story to the next girl. Once everyone has taken a turn, read the scary story you created together aloud!

The bell above the door chimed as I walked through the doorway. I'd always wanted to go into this famous mask shop, but I'd been a little scared at the lifeless faces staring at me from the window. Today I was feeling bold. How I wish I hadn't been. Each mask was scarier than the

next. And the scariest one of all was the one the
mask-maker was carving at that moment . . .

_____

_____

_____

_____

_____

_____

_____

_____

_____

_____

_____

_____

_____

_____

_____

_____

_____

_____

_____

_____

THE END

NEED HELP?
HERE ARE THE ANSWERS

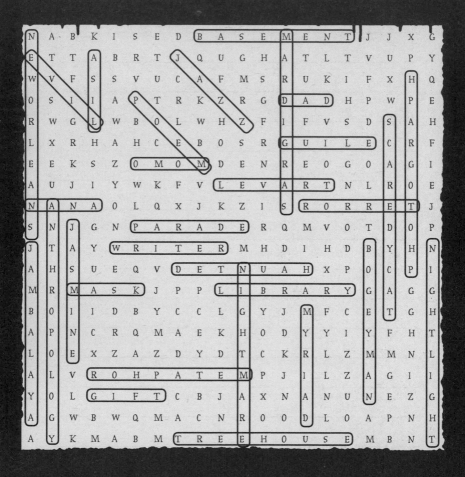

A lifelong night owl, **P. J. NIGHT** often works furiously into the wee hours of the morning, writing down spooky tales and dreaming up new stories of the supernatural and otherworldly. Although P. J.'s whereabouts are unknown at this time, we suspect the author lives in a drafty, old mansion where the floorboards creak when no one is there and the flickering candlelight creates shadows that creep along the walls. We truly wish we could tell you more, but we've been sworn to keep P. J.'s identity a secret . . . and it's a secret we will take to our graves!